MORE THAN A GOVERNESS: A REGENCY ROMANCE

ROSE PEARSON

MORE THAN A GOVERNESS

Ladies on their Own: Governesses and Companions

(Book 4)

By

Rose Pearson

MORE THAN A GOVERNESS

PROLOGUE

"Judith!"

Judith closed her eyes, willing her frustration to die away before she rose from her chair. Rather than send a servant to her, her brother seemed to think it was quite acceptable to roar her name, with as much ferocity as he could, from his study. Hearing her name echoing down the hallway for what was the second time, she took a deep breath and rose from her chair, setting her book aside.

He has become increasingly irritable of late, she thought to herself, walking quickly towards the door, and stepping into the hallway. *During this last year of mourning, he has had naught but a sour disposition and expression whenever he looks at me.* Feeling her stomach begin to knot as she walked to his study, Judith forced her chin upwards and held her head high. Her brother had been in this particular frame of mind ever since he had taken on the title of Viscount Kintore and Judith could not pretend that it had not affected her. It had been a difficult year of mourning and Judith was slowly beginning to lose hope that her brother's countenance would ever improve.

"Yes, brother?"

Stepping into his study without so much as knocking, Judith lifted one eyebrow and looked directly at him, well used to his lowered brow and tight jaw.

"Judith."

Choosing to stand quietly, Judith clasped her hands in front of her and waited.

"You did not make a match last Season."

Blinking quickly, Judith tried to find something to say in response.

"I did not think –"

"I set you in the very best of company and you *still* did not manage to make a match."

"I cannot agree, brother," Judith interrupted, ignoring the red flush which began to creep up her brother's face. "It was well over a year ago – close to eighteen months, in fact. I am certain that your recollection of the Season is a little impaired, given all that has occurred thereafter."

Thumping one hand down flat on his study desk, Lord Kintore half-rose out of his chair.

"I will not be told that my memory is failing!"

"I am not saying anything of the kind," Judith replied, all too aware of the way that her heart began to quicken with fright at his intense reaction. "However, given that it was such a long time ago, and that our father passed shortly thereafter, I hardly think it is fair to lay such a thing at my door now. I have only had one Season!"

Her brother's lip curled.

"That is not an excuse."

Her heart began to pound all the faster at the glint in her brother's eye and the way that his lip continued to pull into an angry sneer. Why was he bringing this up now? Surely there were so many other things to think of, other than the fact that she had not made a match during her first Season? It had been a long time ago and since that time, Judith had done a good deal of thinking on the matter, determined that she would not behave in such a meek and timid fashion again.

"Whilst I am grateful that you placed me in company with Lady Vivian, I shall admit that I found myself incredibly overwhelmed with society itself and the lady's company was.... a little overpowering."

Her brother snorted.

"She was the best introduction to the rest of society *and* for finding a match for yourself - yet you did nothing!"

"I made a sizable number of acquaintances!" Judith protested, ignoring the flush of anger that began to pour into her brother's face. "Father did not insist that I make an immediate match and therefore I used the Season to simply become used to London society."

"But you should have taken the opportunity to make a match," her brother insisted. "Father was unwell, and I made certain to place you in the best possible situation, only for you to fail. Therefore, I have concluded that there is no reason for me to take you back to London for yet another Season."

Judith's hand pressed against her stomach, her whole body turning suddenly cold.

"What do you mean?"

"I have been looking at the finances and the like, and father did not leave this estate in the best situation. To take you to London would be an expense which I fear would be nothing but a frivolous waste."

"That – that is not –"

"So, in a sennight's time, you will make your way across the border to England, to reside with the Marquess of Turton."

Her heart slammed hard against her ribs, causing Judith to gasp aloud.

"I shall not be a... a strumpet! You cannot –"

"You are to be a governess, Judith." Blowing out a long breath of exasperation, Lord Kintore gritted his teeth and glared at her, his jaw working for a few seconds. Subsiding into silence, Judith dropped her head. Her breath seemed to be freezing in her chest, for she was struggling to take in air as her fingers twisted tightly together, but she felt no pain. "The Marquess of Turton seeks a governess for some young girl who now resides with him. I am unaware of the particulars, but I have written to him, and he is now expecting your arrival within a fortnight."

Judith's breath rattled out of her and, try as she might, she could not say a single word. Her mind was attempting to wrap itself around this new situation which she was meant to simply accept, but could not. There was to be no Season. There would not be courtship, marriage, no future husband, children, or house of her own.

She was to be a governess. To look after another person's child and never have the opportunity to bear her own.

And there was nothing she could do but accept it.

CHAPTER ONE

"I hear you are to be congratulated!"

David cleared his throat and tried to smile.

"You hear correctly, old boy." His friend, Lord Carr, arched one eyebrow which David attempted to ignore. "I appreciate your felicitations."

Lord Carr hesitated for a second, glancing back at David as they strolled through the gardens. The warm autumnal wind blew across the path in front of them, a few leaves brushing past their feet, but inwardly David shivered.

"Lady Madeline is a very lovely young lady."

"She is indeed," David agreed, wincing mentally at the haste with which he agreed. "I am certain that I have made an excellent match."

"Good. That is... good."

Lord Carr cleared his throat and David dropped his head, coming to a stop. Taking off his hat, he pushed one hand over his hair and blew out a long, exasperated breath.

"I cannot pretend any longer. You are one of my oldest friends – we have known each other from our Eton days –

and I am quite sure that you are already aware of the truth of the situation."

Lord Carr grinned, his eyes twinkling, making David scowl.

"Ah, and now I am to have the truth."

"You already know it, I am sure."

Shrugging one shoulder, Lord Carr's grin only spread.

"I may. Might it be that your betrothal has come about rather hastily?" Closing his eyes, David pulled his lips to one side. "You were only introduced a little over a month ago, was it not?"

"Six weeks, to be precise."

"And now you are betrothed."

Throwing up his hands, David exclaimed aloud.

"It was a little hasty, yes! But it was the end of the Season, and I was aware of the expectation and therefore, when it came time for our final parting, I felt such..." Trailing off, he took in a deep breath and tried to find the words. Throwing back his head, he let out another sigh, screwing up his eyes. "She was tearful and, I confess, such beauty and sorrow intertwined tore at my heart, so that before I realized what I was saying, I was betrothed."

Dropping his head back, he saw his friend's smile fade.

"I am sorry."

"I – I am going to convince myself that I have made the very best of matches," David said, speaking with more firmness than before, in an attempt to persuade himself. "It was a little hasty, yes but that does not mean that it is doomed to failure."

"Of course not." Lord Carr clapped him on the shoulder and together, they continued back towards the house. "Lady Madeline comes from good stock. Her father and mother are both from excellent families and you clearly found her genteel and elegant. Her conversation is good and her company quite exhilarating?"

David cleared his throat.

"I did not grow weary during our conversations, few as they were," he confessed, choosing to speak openly to his friend and not hold anything back from him. "However, I will admit to you that I found her beauty to be more than a little overwhelming."

Lord Carr's mouth tugged to one side.

"She is a diamond of the first water, I suppose."

"She has been called that, certainly and it is not a compliment which I would disagree with."

"Then you think that you will be satisfied with your choice?"

David hesitated, chewing his lip.

"I – I think I must hope so."

"There is no way that you could end your current situation?"

Shaking his head, David tried to smile, but his lips refused to curl.

"You know very well that a gentleman cannot end his betrothal without causing scandal. I would not risk that. The damage it would cause to the lady's reputation would be severe, and I would not escape scandal either. If there was some great concern over the betrothal, or the lady herself, then I would certainly bring the betrothal to an end but, given that she is a diamond of the first water, I cannot see any reason to even *consider* ending our betrothal."

Lord Carr's lip curled, his expression wry and his eyes narrowing gently.

"It sounds as though you are attempting to convince yourself of such a thing, old boy."

"Perhaps I am." Sighing, David ran one hand over his

eyes. "As you are aware, the house party will begin in a few days and I am certain that, once I am again in her company, I will have no concerns whatsoever."

"Indeed." Lord Carr smiled but his eyes did not brighten. "I am grateful to you for a prolonged visit, and I must hope that you will not mind my presence at your house party also."

David chuckled, finally able to push back his concerns for the present.

"You have been excellent company and I do not think that the house party would be as lively without you!" His small smile faded. "And the governess is due to arrive shortly also. I must hope that she will appear before the house party begins, else the servants may struggle with their split responsibilities."

Lord Carr threw him a quick, questioning glance, his hands behind his back as they meandered back to the house.

"And how is the child?"

"Silent." David grimaced. "The governess *must* make her speak, for I shall not be content with a mute daughter!"

"Little Laura has been through a great ordeal. Mayhap she finds the loss of her mother to be an ongoing burden."

David shook his head, snorting his discontent.

"I hardly think so. The girl is only five years of age and given that my wife passed some three years ago, I do not think that she will remember much about her."

Lord Carr cleared his throat, his brow furrowing, although he did not look across at David.

"But you recall that she did not know of you, however. Given that you left her and your late wife to live quietly in another house whilst you remained here, you must consider the effect that will have had on her."

Aware of the twisting of his stomach as his thoughts

were unwillingly turned towards his late wife, David scowled.

"I had every reason to set my wife there. I felt I had no choice."

"I am well aware of that, and I am always grateful to you for your willingness to speak to me of it, given that it was such a sensitive matter."

"I trust you implicitly, Carr."

"And I am greatly appreciative of that trust. And I should tell you that I believe you did the right thing in setting her there." Coughing, Lord Carr shook his head. "Perhaps you are right. The governess will know what to do. I am sure that your daughter will be much improved by the time the house party ends."

"My Lord?"

The butler stepped into David's study; his hands clasped lightly in front of him as he waited for David's request.

"My daughter."

David did not look up from where he was writing but kept his gaze fixed on his desk.

"Yes, my Lord?"

"Did she speak today?"

A short silence followed the question and David closed his eyes briefly, all too aware of the answer.

"I do not believe so, my Lord. There may have been one or two words to the maid but nothing by way of conversation."

Setting down his quill, David looked up at his butler, his jaw set.

"How long has the girl resided here with me?"

"A little over three months, my Lord."

David nodded slowly to himself.

"I should have found a governess more quickly."

A slight stab of conscience lodged itself in his heart, but he dismissed it quickly. Whilst his wife had passed some three years ago, David had not taken his daughter into his home until a few months ago. Telling himself that it would be best for the girl to remain in the small house where she had lived with her mother, he had made certain that the child had nursemaids, maids, and various other staff to care for her, whilst he continued to reside in the manor house. His conscience had been soothed by the daily reports he had received from his staff as to her welfare, and by telling himself that his excursions and his trips away to London for both business and company meant that he would not be of any benefit to the girl. But the child had reached the age where a governess was required and thus, David had chosen to bring her into his house.

Except that the child had said not a single word to him since her arrival. In fact, she had fallen quite silent even with those whom she knew well. David had hoped that this would soon change, but it seemed that his daughter was quite determined to remain mute.

"Is there something else that you require?" The butler lifted his gaze a fraction, although it hovered somewhere around David's left shoulder. "Should I bring your daughter to you?"

"No." Picking up his quill, David waved his other hand dismissively. "There is nothing else." Hearing the butler open the door, David recalled something. "Wait a moment, if you please." Lifting his eyes, he held his butler's gaze for a few moments. "The very second that the governess arrives, I want her brought directly to me. Is that clear?"

The butler nodded.

"But of course."

"I do not want to hear that she was greatly fatigued and therefore required a little rest before she came to my door. I do not give two figs as to how weary the governess is, I *must* see her the very moment that she arrives. I have much to explain as regards my daughter, and would prefer that she hear of it all from the very beginning, *before* any particular impression can be made."

The butler nodded again, but David narrowed his eyes slightly. One thing he knew about his staff was that they were inclined to talk, to gossip, and would, no doubt, say something to the governess as regarded either himself as the master of the house, or his daughter. That was not something which David wished for. The moment the governess arrived, David would make certain that she heard about his daughter and her situation from his own lips, rather than from the whispers of a maid.

"But of course, my Lord."

"Very good. You are dismissed."

David waited until the door closed behind the butler before setting his quill down. Pressing his head back against his chair, he closed his eyes and let his huff of breath escape loudly.

I am much too overcome. I have my mute daughter, my uncertain betrothal, the house party, and the governess who, as yet, is still absent. My mind is heavy indeed.

Opening his eyes, David ran one hand over his face and pushed himself back up so that his arms rested on his desk once more. Picking up his quill, he read over what he had written, scowling as he did so.

"I cannot falsify sentiment which I do not feel."

Muttering to himself, David quickly penned the final few words and then signed his name. His heart did not lift, and no joyous sentiment filled him. The letter he was responding to had been from his betrothed, filled with exclamations of delight and murmurs of love – none of which David himself felt. She had expressed her eagerness for the house party, almost desperate in her desire to be in his company again and yet David was all too aware of his lack of sentiment in that regard. These last few weeks away from the lady had been a time of relief that had brought with it a sense of freedom – albeit a freedom which was false in nature, given that he was now tied to Lady Madeline. No plans for their wedding had been made but, no doubt, those discussions would be expected once she was here within his house. A house which she would soon expect to be mistress of.

"What have I done?" Groaning, David pushed one hand through his thick, dark hair and let himself fall back in his chair once more. He had been much too hasty. Overwhelmed by her beauty and caught by her obvious expectation and, in truth, his desire for her continued company, he had spoken without any real consideration and now found himself betrothed and doubtful that he had made the right choice. Lord Carr was right. David did not know the lady's character particularly well and, whilst she came from a good family and certainly appeared to be all that a lady ought to be, that did not mean that they would be a good match. "It is not as though I revealed a great deal of my character to her, either."

Still muttering darkly to himself, David closed his eyes and let out another long, heavy sigh. There was no use deliberating with himself. The matter was settled. He had proposed, she had accepted and whilst her father had been a little perturbed that David had not asked his explicit permission beforehand, the match was made.

There was nothing for it. Within the next few months, he would find himself wed to Lady Madeline, a lady he knew very little about, indeed. But doubts or concerns meant nothing, for he could not step away now - the lady was to be his wife, and mistress of his estate and the sooner he came to accept that, the better.

Leaning forward, David dusted his letter, folded it up, and began to warm the wax to seal it. His jaw tightened and his brow furrowed as he completed the note, setting it to one side for the time being. There was no urgency for it to be sent to the lady, else he feared she would return him another letter before the house party, and he would then have to express all manner of delight to her about it, given that he would not have time to reply.

"My Lord?"

The butler rapped lightly at the door, urgency in his voice.

"Yes?"

The door opened and the butler stepped in, his expression a little pinched.

"My Lord, the governess has arrived."

A little surprised, David rose at once from his chair.

"Do send her in!" Relief swept over him, pushing away his thoughts on Lady Madeline for the present. "That is fortunate indeed!"

Stepping to one side, the butler extended an arm, and, after a moment, a young lady walked into the room.

David's heart slammed against his ribs and his breath seemed to lodge itself in his chest.

This creature, a governess?

The lady was dressed in a navy gown with a high neck, but lacking a little embellishment at the sleeves and neckline. Her red hair was pulled back neatly into a chignon, and thus she appeared just as any governess ought.

But it was not her dress which caught David's attention. This young lady's blue eyes were vivid and bright, looking all about the room before turning their attention to him. There was no sense of fear in her expression, no attempt at setting her gaze to one side, as any servant might do. David swallowed hard, aware that his own gaze had been making its way lightly down her form, snapping it back to her face once more. Her gentle nose had a light smattering of freckles across it – a feature which was meant to be unsightly to many a gentleman but David, much to his surprise, did not think it at all ugly. Her full lips curved gently into a small smile, but it did not warm her eyes. They remained a little cold.

"Lord Turton. I am –"

"Miss Abernathy, yes. I am aware." He saw her blink, the faint hint of color in her cheeks quickly fading. "Lord Kintore informed me of your background and your situation. I am sure that, given that your last charge was so pleased with your instruction, there shall be no difficulties here." Her eyes fluttered and her teeth nipped out to catch her bottom lip, but she remained entirely silent. "Please, sit down. There is much I need to speak to you about, before you meet my daughter." Waiting for the lady to take her seat, David observed a slight tremble catching her frame and felt a small twinge of guilt. "Tea, Burch." The butler nodded and stepped out of the room, leaving David and his new governess alone. Satisfied that she, at least, had arrived, David sat back in his chair and took in a deep breath. "Now, let me explain."

CHAPTER TWO

Judith clasped her hands together in front of her, her nerves growing steadily as she waited for the butler to speak to Lord Turton before admitting her. The journey had been long and arduous, and she had found herself greatly distressed for a good deal of it. Struggling to keep her emotions in check whilst she had been driven to Lord Turton's estate, Judith had felt everything begin to crumple within her. Her brother had thrown her from his estate, had left her in a situation where she was now to be a governess with no chance of ever marrying, simply because he did not wish for her to be any sort of financial burden to his seemingly already pressed coffers. Silently, Judith had listed the various different things that her brother might have given up, instead of sending her away – perhaps selling some of his many, *many* horses, reducing his frequent trips to London or Bath, and mayhap even choosing not to purchase new clothing every month or so - but that, it seemed, had not even been a consideration.

"Come in, please."

Jolted out of her reverie, Judith looked up at the butler,

who was now standing to one side, holding one hand out towards the door. Stammering her thanks, she walked into the study, finding herself quite overcome.

What can a Marquess be thinking, hiring a lady of such distinction as a governess? Her chin lifted as she stepped into the Marquess' presence, her jaw tight as her heart began to pound. She did not know exactly what her brother had told him, but she certainly had no reputation as a governess! It was very strange indeed that a Marquess should be so eager to hire the daughter of a Viscount, especially when she had no experience as a governess.

Looking up, she took in Lord Turton, finding herself balking just a little at his somewhat formidable presence. He was not an old man but seemed to be of an age with her brother, although he was dark-haired where her brother was fair. Light grey eyes flared a little, as though he were surprised to see her. Was he waiting for her to speak?

Placing her hands behind her, her fingers twining together, Judith cleared her throat gently.

"Lord Turton. I am –"

"Miss Abernathy, yes. I am aware."

Judith blinked at his somewhat sharp retort, squeezing her fingers tightly together. *Miss Abernathy?* That was not her name nor her title – whyever was Lord Turton referring to her in such a way? Perhaps he was mistaken. Mayhap he was thinking her to be someone else, or the butler had mistaken her title for that of another. It was on the tip of her tongue to say something more, when Lord Turton spoke again.

"Lord Kintore informed me of your background and your situation. I am sure, given that your last charge was so pleased with your instruction, that there shall be no difficulties here."

Shock rolled through her, and she caught her breath. Biting her lip, Judith took in another breath and let it out slowly, choosing to remain entirely silent rather than correct him.

It seemed that her brother had told nothing but lies. Lord Turton did not know of her true status nor her connection to her brother. She'd had no previous charge. There was no real reputation to speak of. Everything that her brother had told Lord Turton was, it seemed, untrue.

"Please, sit down. There is much I need to speak to you about, before you meet my daughter."

Having no other recourse but to do so, Judith sat, aware of the slight tremble in her frame.

"Tea, Burch."

Closing her eyes for a moment, Judith tried to breathe deeply but felt her chest tighten.

"You must be very grateful to your cousin."

Her eyes flickered open.

"Cousin?"

Lord Turton nodded.

"To Lord Kintore, of course."

Judith hesitated. Ought she to tell him the truth now? Her brother would not be pleased with her, but Judith could not simply continue on in Lord Turton's home with such a falsehood hanging over her. Her courage was severely lacking, but Judith lifted her chin, tightened her hands together in her lap and looked directly into Lord Turton's eyes.

"Lord Kintore is not my cousin, Lord Turton."

The man blinked in surprise.

"I beg your pardon?"

"Lord Kintore is my brother." Her Scottish lilt felt thick on her lips. "I am deeply sorry to have to tell you such a thing, but I will not have his mistruths hang over my head. I will not pretend to be someone that I am not. I will not reside in your household under a false name and false pretenses when I know them to be so." Her voice was shaking but Judith forced words from her lips. "My name is Miss Judith Newfield, daughter to the late Viscount Kintore."

Lord Turton's grey eyes turned to dark slate, his jaw tightening discernibly. One clenched fist pressed hard to his mouth as he turned his eyes away from her, and yet she heard the huff of breath that escaped him. Lowering her head, Judith winced against the sudden pain in her chest as her heart began to race. Waiting for the Marquess' reaction, she pressed her elbows into her sides, keeping her head low and her hands clasped tightly in her lap.

"Lord Kintore is your brother." Lord Turton's voice was rasping as if he could not quite believe what she had told him. "Your *brother*."

"Yes."

"Then I have hired a Viscount's daughter to be my child's governess. A lady!"

Her stomach tugged furiously from one side to the other as she dared a look at him. The man was white-faced, save for a dot of redness on each cheek.

"That is so, Lord Turton. I must apologize profusely, for even I did not know what my brother had said of me." Her shoulders lifted in a small shrug, a strange, unsettling laugh pulling from her lips as she twined her fingers together again. "When you addressed me as Miss Abernathy, I could not fathom –"

"But you knew that he sent you here to be a governess?"

Lord Turton's voice was hard, and Judith flinched visibly.

"Yes, of course. I am aware of the situation I am stepping into, Lord Turton, although I know very little of the child I am to care for."

"I see." Lord Turton ran one hand over his chin, turning his head away as he looked out towards the large windows to his left. The thickness of the air began to swirl around Judith, making it suddenly exceedingly difficult to catch her breath. Would he send her away? Return her to her brother? The thought sent a dart of fear straight through Judith's heart and she closed her eyes, pressing her lips together as she fought back the first hints of panic. If she was returned to her brother, then Judith could not imagine what his response would be. Yes, she had done the right thing in telling Lord Turton the truth, but that, she was sure, would mean very little to Lord Kintore. He would be angry with her. *Furious*, even. And what plans he would have for her thereafter would, no doubt, be even worse that her current situation. "You have had your own governess, I assume?" Lord Turton's sharp voice pulled Judith out of her thoughts. "You have all of the necessary accomplishments required of a lady?" A slight lift of her chin answered Lord Turton's question before she could put words to it. "I do not understand why your brother should send you away, Miss Newfield. I should hope that it is not because of anything... unseemly."

Heat seared her cheeks.

"I can assure you that it is not." Hearing the tightness and the slight bite to her words, Judith sat up a little straighter in her chair. "Lord Turton, my brother sent me away because he does not wish for me to be a financial burden upon him, and for no other reason than that."

"Then why did he not tell me the truth of your situation?"

Judith spread her hands.

"Would you have been willing to hire me, had you known it?" The silence which followed gave her the answer and she shook her head, aware of the ache in her throat and the growing swell of tears behind her eyes. "My brother did not wish me to remain in his house for a single day longer than was required. Therefore, he wished to have me removed as quickly as possible and saw this to be one way forward. I assume that he did not expect me to tell you the truth of the situation but instead expected me to simply accept it, for fear of incurring your wrath as well as his own, should I speak honestly."

Lord Turton cleared his throat gruffly, shifting a little in his chair. The door opened before he could speak and a maid hurried in with the tea tray, which was quickly set down in front of Judith before the maid escaped the room again without so much as a word. Evidently, the staff were well used to doing as Lord Turton asked without question and without hesitation.

And now what is to become of me?

Looking up at Lord Turton, she saw him eye the tea tray, as though offering it to her would be an acceptance of her presence here. Another gentle cough and he shook his head grimly.

"Very well, Miss Newfield." Blinking quickly, a gasp lodged itself in her chest. "You shall stay and be my daughter's governess. As you have had all of the necessary training, I have every expectation that you shall do all that is required."

Stammering a little, Judith tried to smile.

"Certainly, Lord Turton. I shall do my absolute best for your daughter."

Hearing Lord Turton's harrumph, Judith swallowed

hard and dropped her gaze. She had no experience of being a governess and yet, she found herself strangely grateful. The thought of returning to her brother and informing him that she had been sent home again by the Marquess was rather frightening, given that Judith was certain she would have faced a great deal of anger.

"Please, pour the tea." The Marquess sat back in his chair and steepled his fingers. "I have a house party next week, Miss Newfield, and require a governess for my daughter by then, or else I may well have made an entirely different decision." Judith frowned, but did not respond, reaching to pour the tea for herself, given that there was only one cup on the tea tray. "My daughter is young and has only recently returned to my house."

"Oh?"

Judith lifted her head, seeing the flash in Lord Turton's eyes at her response, but she did not find herself at all embarrassed at having asked such a thing. If she was to be the child's governess, then it was best for her to know the full extent of the girl's situation.

"My late wife and my daughter resided in another house, a short distance from my estate."

Lord Turton looked away, his chin lifting a fraction as Judith battled to keep the astonishment from her expression. Why would a gentleman do such a thing as that?

"When my wife passed away, my daughter was still very young and, given that I was very often away from my own house, I thought it best that she remain there for a time, surrounded by the staff that she knew and the familiar situation."

Judith blinked in surprise but focused her gaze on her cup of tea, rather than allow Lord Turton to read her expression. The last thing which was required at this point was for him to be aware of her shock at such a situation! Her heart twisted, however, and she let out a slow, surreptitious breath, rather sorry that such a small child should have been left in such a situation.

"Given that she now requires a governess, I made the arrangements for her to reside here instead."

"I see." After sipping delicately at her tea, Judith set the cup down carefully onto the saucer. "And has she settled in?"

One eyebrow lifted gently but was met with a deep frown that had Judith's soft smile fading.

"My daughter does not speak." Lord Turton's words were harsh and dark, demanding her silence even though a torrent of questions flung themselves to her lips. "She remains mute. I believe that, on occasion, she has whispered to her nurse, but she will not speak to either myself or any other staff."

Judith nodded slowly, allowing herself to search Lord Turton's expression. It was clear that he was angry that he was unable to communicate with his daughter, although quite why that was, Judith did not know. It could be that he was embarrassed that the child would not speak and afraid that society would discover it. Or it might be that he regretted leaving the child in her late mother's home for so long, and wished he had done differently. Or it might be, simply, that he had tried and failed to have his daughter converse with him.

"She spoke animatedly to her late mother and, thereafter, to the staff at the house she resided in. However, since removing to *this* house, she has fallen quite silent."

"And you wish me to make her speak?"

Lord Turton threw up his hands.

"But of course! I do not wish to have a daughter who will not speak to another living soul, save for her nurse!"

"I see."

A slight tremble ran down Judith's frame, but she did not let the fear take hold of her just yet. This was a difficult enough situation already and now, for him to have presented her with another complication of such magnitude threatened to quite overwhelm her – but Judith knew that she could not permit fear to shake her at present, not in front of Lord Turton. Picking up her teacup, she sipped at it again and allowed the hot tea to spread warmth through her chest, freeing her a little.

"It will take time, and I will permit you that, of course. But I expect to be able to speak with my daughter very soon." Judith said nothing. Finishing her cup of tea, she set it down on the saucer and took in a deep breath, straightening her shoulders. Suddenly, everything felt more than a little overwhelming. There was a lot of responsibility now settled on her shoulders and, even though she was attempting to keep her fears and worries in check, Judith could not deny that she worried that she would fail completely. "Once you have had time to rest and refresh yourself a little more, you will meet my daughter. The housekeeper will arrange it."

A little surprised, Judith's eyebrows lifted, but she did not say anything in response. For Lord Turton not to introduce his own daughter to her new governess was not only surprising, it also lacked any sort of consideration for the girl herself. No doubt, the child would be afraid, uncertain, and unsure - but it was to be the *housekeeper* rather than her father who introduced her? That made very little sense to Judith's mind.

"I will have a footman show you to..." Wincing, Lord

Turton cleared his throat. "The governess' quarters will not be what you are used to, Miss Newfield. I am certain that they can be improved but, for the present, they will have to do."

"I quite understand."

"Good." Gesturing to the door, Lord Turton waited until Judith had risen to her feet before he reached to ring the bell. "If you would wait in the hall, Miss Newfield, the footman will be with you in a moment."

Being sent from Lord Turton's presence as though she were a servant stabbed hard at Judith's pride, but she merely nodded and made her way to the door.

I am not a servant, but neither am I his equal, she reminded herself as a dull flush began to creep up her chest and into her face, making her turn all the more hastily towards the door. *I must learn my new place in his household and accept it without difficulty.*

Making her way out of the study, Judith pulled the door closed and stood quietly to one side, her hands clasped lightly in front of her. Whether or not the governess' quarters would be suitable for her or not, Judith did not care. All she wanted for the present was simply to be on her own, so that she might come to terms with her new situation and consider all of the responsibility which had been placed on her shoulders. The fear that she would fail, that the girl would not so much as look at her, let alone speak, as her father wished, began to grow like a great, menacing shadow that she could not push away, and Judith dropped her head, fighting against sudden, hot tears. Everything was changed and she could never again return to the life she had once enjoyed.

There was no going back now.

CHAPTER THREE

"And has the governess' arrival made any difference to your daughter?"

David grimaced, then shrugged.

"I could not say."

Lord Carr lifted one eyebrow.

"You do not know?"

"No, I do not. It has not yet come into my consideration." A huff of breath escaped Lord Carr as he shook his head, obviously rather surprised, and David tried to ignore the small prickle of guilt that followed upon observing his friend's reaction. "I have been busy," he continued, speaking rather quickly. "The house party has required additional planning and given that the first of my guests is to arrive at any moment, I have found myself quite distracted."

"I see."

Lord Carr did not sound at all convinced, but David continued on, shrugging his shoulders as though he truly did not care.

"My daughter will be quite content with the new governess, I am sure. There has been no concern nor complaint brought to me by any of the other staff and, therefore, I am quite certain that all is well."

Lord Carr reached for his brandy glass, took a sip, and then tilted his head a fraction, his sharp eyes studying David.

"And you are satisfied with the governess herself? You have confidence in her?"

Wincing, David shook his head.

"I would not say that I have confidence in her, no. More that I have no other choice but to keep her on, given that there was not enough time between her arrival and the beginning of the house party to hire someone else."

"Whatever is wrong?"

Lord Carr's eyes were wide with astonishment and David gave his friend a wry smile.

"She is not Miss Abernathy, as I was told. She has not, in fact, been governess to anyone before, and certainly does not have any record!"

"But – but you were told precisely of such a thing, were you not? Lord Kintore –"

"Lord Kintore has sent his own sister to be my daughter's governess." David's lips tugged into a wry smile at Lord Carr's astonished gasp. "Indeed, I was as shocked as you when she first told me of it."

"She *told* you that she was not Miss Abernathy?"

"Indeed, she did. All was carefully and quickly explained and, whilst I found myself angry and frustrated with Lord Kintore for behaving so, I could not, I decided, refuse to hire the lady, and send her home. My daughter requires a governess, and she is a lady who has been trained in all the required accomplishments, given that she will have had a governess also, as she grew up."

Lord Carr let out a low whistle, shaking his head to himself, his gaze away from David.

"Good gracious."

"It did come as something of a surprise, I confess it."

"Although you must have been impressed with her gumption."

David considered for a moment, then nodded.

"Yes, I believe I was. I am sure that, had I returned her to her brother, there would have been a great deal of anger for her to face, given Lord Kintore's manipulation of the situation in the first place, and I did not want her to have to face that."

His friend's eyebrow lifted, and a tightness came into his smile.

"Besides, you needed a governess in time for the house party, did you not?" Aware of the prickling of his conscience and the fact that, had it not been for the house party, David would have simply sent Miss Newfield back to her brother, David picked up his brandy glass and threw the final mouthful back, choosing not to answer his friend's question. "I do hope that the lady is all that you require," Lord Carr finished. "I must say, I do feel rather sorry for her. To be thrown into this particular situation without any say in the matter must be very difficult indeed."

"It will take time for her to become used to the situation, certainly," David agreed, "but that cannot be helped. As I have said, I have received no complaint from any of my staff and there have been no concerns raised about the lady. I am sure it will all work out very well."

Lord Carr set down his glass on the small table near the fireplace, then began to wander across the room towards the window.

"You will not send her home once the house party has finished, then?"

"Not unless I have reason to."

"I see." Lord Carr's hands coupled behind his back as he looked out across the grounds. "You will, of course, make sure that she remains away from the guests during the house party? It would be something of a humiliation, I am sure, for her to be seen in her present situation, given that it might then spread to the rest of society."

That is not a consideration that had even entered my head.

"But of course, that would be wise." David tried to pretend that he did not feel a stab of guilt over his lack of consideration and walked across the room to join his friend. "There is no reason for me to present either her or my daughter to my guests. I am certain that they themselves will be very glad indeed to be kept away from others."

"Indeed." Another lift of the eyebrow. "And Lady Madeline?"

"I expect she and her mother will be amongst the first to arrive," David replied, keeping any hint of displeasure from his voice. "I managed to send her a reply to her letter which I must hope she has received before she left to journey here."

"Ah, I think you are quite correct, Turton!" Lord Carr tapped the window with one finger. "Look, is there not a carriage arriving?"

David narrowed his eyes, seeing the cloud of dust being blown up from what would be a set of carriage wheels.

"It may not be Lady Madeline," he said, turning on his heel. "Although I must make my way to the front of the house to greet them, whoever it might be."

"I will remain here, I think." Lord Carr grinned as

David straightened his jacket and tugged lightly on both sleeves, making certain that he looked his best. "I should not want to interrupt your reconnection with Lady Madeline."

"If it is even her carriage," David muttered, not looking at his friend, but hurrying towards the door. "I will return to you soon. No doubt whoever is inside will wish for a short time to rest after their journey."

Lord Carr said nothing, but swung back to the window, leaving David to walk from the library towards the staircase. Just as he reached it, he heard another, somewhat unfamiliar voice calling his name.

"Lord Turton? Pray excuse me, but I was coming in search of you so that–"

Miss Newfield. It had been some days since he had last laid eyes on her but now was not the time for conversation.

"Excuse me, Miss Newfield, but I cannot stop to speak with you. I have guests arriving."

She put one hand on the staircase rail, looking back at him steadily as he approached, her jaw tightening imperceptibly.

"I have come to speak with you on two previous occasions, Lord Turton, but you have been quite unavailable."

"I do not recall–" David's eyes flared in surprise when she stepped forward, blocking his access to the staircase. "Miss Newfield, I hardly think–"

"When is it that I might come to speak with you about your daughter?" Her voice was clear and her blue eyes alive with determination. "I wished to do so yesterday but you were unable to speak with me both in the morning and later in the afternoon. Do you not recall?"

David grimaced, not wanting to push his way past the lady but finding her insistence on speaking with him when he had made it clear that he could not do so at present to be more than a little infuriating.

"I asked the footman to ask you on both occasions. The message I received in return was that you were much too busy and could not speak with me at present. This morning, I did the same again but was informed that you had no time during this day either."

"I have guests arriving, Miss Newfield, and –"

"Does everything come before your daughter, Lord Turton?"

David's mouth fell open as his eyes flared wide in astonishment. Miss Newfield, however, showed neither remorse nor embarrassment and continued to look back at him steadily, with her arms now folding across her chest and one eyebrow lifting.

Lost for what he was to say in response, David stared back into her eyes, immediately beginning to regret the fact that he had ever hired the daughter of a Viscount as his governess. He ought to have sent her back home, for he was quite sure that no hired governess with experience of such a position would have *ever* spoken to him in such a way.

"My Lord?" The butler stood at the bottom of the staircase, looking up at him. "I beg your pardon for interrupting, but a carriage is about to arrive."

David gave him a swift nod.

"Yes, I saw. I shall come to greet my guests." Turning his head back towards Miss Newfield, he saw her shake her head, her gaze now falling to the floor. "Miss Newfield." Lifting his shoulders, he stood straight and tall, his hands at his hips and his gaze a little narrowed. "I shall allow this indiscretion to pass only once, given that you are not accustomed to the station of a governess." Taking a small step closer to her, he saw her eyes lift to his and hold his gaze steadily once more. A tightness curled about his heart, squeezing it rather painfully as a flash of anger speared his mind. Miss Newfield did not seem at all perturbed by what she had said nor by how she had behaved. "You do not get to demand when I speak with you, Miss Newfield." Keeping his voice low, David moved even closer. "You may very well have my daughter's best interests in mind, but I am a gentleman with much to consider. There are many responsibilities and obligations which are for my shoulders alone to bear – something that I do not think the daughter of a Viscount could understand, given that your life will have been one of leisure."

He had not meant the sneering tone to come into his voice, but the sudden glistening in her eyes told him that it was there and that she had not only heard it but felt it also. The sting of his conscience had an apology springing to his lips, but the lady spoke before he could say anything.

"You may believe, my Lord, that there is nothing in your current position which I might understand and, mayhap in some ways, that is true." Now it was her turn to move closer so that they were only a few inches apart. Her chin lifted, her head tilted back, and her sharp eyes demanded his full attention, even though David knew that the carriage would now be pulling up to the front of the house. He was caught by Miss Newfield's gaze, forced to linger when he ought to depart. "However, Lord Turton, *I* have been the forgotten daughter. The one who did not merit much attention at all, who was left without company or conversation, or even responsibility. I am the sister who has been deemed a burden and who has been thrust out of the only home I have ever known, at the whim of my gentleman brother. Do not think, Lord Turton, that I have no understanding of burden. It may be different from your own, but it is still very much a heavy weight. And it is one I should not wish to settle on the shoulders of your daughter."

Everything that David wanted to say in response seemed to dry up on his lips. The words she had spoken began to cut deeply into his heart, sending a stabbing guilt into his conscience. For whatever reason, he could not seem to pull his gaze from hers. There were hints of grey in her eyes also, merging into the blue. Did that shade only appear when she was angry? When she was upset? His shoulders dropped as the sound of her quickened breathing caught his ears, making him realize just how fast his heart was racing. He wanted to step back but found his feet fastened to the ground, refusing to shift even a little. The color in Miss Newfield's cheeks heightened as he licked his lips, struggling to find something to say, something which would break this foolish tension that bound them both together so tightly.

"My Lord, Lady Heslington and Lady Madeline have arrived."

The voice of the footman startled David, making him jerk, but it was what was needed for him to be finally pulled away from Miss Newfield. He could not give any easy explanation for what had happened, nor for why he found himself so drawn to the lady but, relieved that he was freed from her gaze now, David turned away directly.

"But of course."

Without so much as a backwards glance, he began to hurry down the staircase towards the front door, which was already being opened by his two footmen. No doubt Lady Heslington would have been a little disappointed that he had not been waiting on the steps for them to alight from the carriage, but he could, at least, merely pretend that he had been waiting for some time indoors, ready to greet them the moment they stepped inside.

"Lady Heslington and Lady Madeline, my Lord."

The butler announced their arrival and bowed low as the ladies walked into the foyer. David stepped forward at once, greeting both of the ladies quickly but noticing, much to his dismay, that he did not have any quickening of his heart as regarded Lady Madeline's presence. In fact, as he looked at her, smiling up at him as she rose from her curtsey, David found that his heart was filled with nothing but distinct dread. She was as beautiful as ever, yet the prospect of once more being in her company, of being often in conversation with her, left him with a sinking heart and a sudden desire to escape from her entirely.

"Welcome to my home." Forcing a smile to his lips, he offered Lady Madeline his arm which, of course, she accepted without hesitation. "Come, allow me to show you briefly around the house itself and, thereafter, you will want to refresh and rest yourself, of course."

"I need no rest, not now that I am back in company with you," Lady Madeline murmured, as David glanced at her, seeing the flare of excitement in her eyes. "You cannot know just how long I have waited for this moment, Lord Turton."

David smiled briefly but, as he turned, ready to lead Lady Madeline through the house, his attention caught suddenly on the figure at the top of the staircase.

Miss Newfield.

Lady Madeline and her mother were already beginning to talk about just how marvelous his house was, even though they were yet to leave the foyer, but David could not seem to give the conversation even the smallest consideration. Instead, he let his regard fix upon Miss Newfield, noting how her gaze roved from himself to Lady Madeline and back again, although she did not catch his eye. A sadness enveloped her, for her shoulders slumped and her head lowered suddenly, until she turned sharply away.

A heaviness seemed to flow down the stairs from her and twist itself around David's shoulders as he grimaced. Miss Newfield was the daughter of a Viscount and, by all accounts, should be eagerly looking forward to London and the Season. Instead, she was now a hired governess, forced into the shadows instead of being able to step forward into the place she had, by rights, so often taken before.

"Lord Turton?"

Starting, he looked down into the confused face of Lady Madeline, seeing her eyes widen slightly.

"Forgive me, my dear. I was lost in thought about how wonderful these next few days are to be." That seemed to be the right thing to say, for Lady Madeline beamed at him and her hand tightened a little on his arm. "Come, allow me to lead you down the hallway so that we might see the drawing-room."

"And you must show me the ballroom, for I am hopeful that you will have a ball at the end of the house party?"

David nodded, hearing Lady Madeline's contented sigh.

"But of course. Please."

Gesturing with his other hand, he began to walk purposefully towards the drawing-room but, try as he might, his thoughts lingered solely on Miss Newfield rather than on the important company he now kept. His jaw tight, David scowled, turning his head away so that Lady Madeline would not see. Remembering the conversation which had taken place before Lady Madeline's arrival, David's irritation rose once again. Miss Newfield truly was a most frustrating young lady, and he would, no matter what, make certain that she knew her place and kept to it – even if he *did* have a little sympathy for her present circumstance. The only thing which was required of her was to look after his daughter and make her speak. Nothing else was of any importance, and David told himself sternly that he need not think of the lady any longer.

CHAPTER FOUR

Watching Lord Turton offer the lady his arm had sent Judith into such an emotional state that it had taken all of her strength to hide the tears which wanted so desperately to fall. Her gaze had wanted to linger on the scene, putting herself in the position of Lady Madeline, knowing that she had every right to be in amongst them and yet finding herself resigned to her current circumstances. Lord Turton had made his expectations of her situation abundantly clear given how he had practically reprimanded her – although Judith knew, deep in her heart, that he had every right to do so, given the manner in which she had spoken.

I do not yet fully understand my place.

Her footsteps echoed along the hallway as she hurried back towards her bedchamber, opposite the schoolroom. Lady Laura, her charge, had been taken for a short walk out of doors, before the guests arrived for the house party but, given that the first carriage had already made its way to the house, Judith knew that the child and the maid would soon be returning. Rubbing one hand over her eyes, she made her way into the schoolroom, closing the door behind her so that she would not be disturbed.

And then, the tears came.

Pressing both hands down onto the desk, with rounded shoulders and head bowed low, Judith let her tears flow without restraint. Her frame shook gently as the tears dripped onto her cheeks and then fell to the table. Making no attempt to wipe them away, Judith sobbed openly, struggling against her overwhelming emotions. She had not cried – not even once - since her brother had informed her of her new situation, and it was only now, some days after her arrival at Lord Turton's manor house, that she was finally able to do so. For whatever reason, seeing him walk with Lady Madeline, seeing him welcoming his guests, had torn straight through her heart, rendering her quite broken.

And I cannot make the girl speak.

Having spent only a few days in Lady Laura's company, Judith found herself more lost than ever before. The child did not speak, did not utter a single word and yet Lord Turton expected her to be able to make some sort of progress with the girl's education? It seemed to be a great impossibility, especially given that she had very little idea of what she ought to do. Had she actually been a governess with experience, then she might, at the very least, have had one or two ideas - but nothing came to mind. Given her lack of insight, Judith had wanted to speak to Lord Turton to ask him specifically what had been tried already, and what he might suggest but as yet, he seemed quite unwilling to give her even a few minutes of his time.

"I am lost."

Her broken whisper only added to her pain and Judith sniffed, forced to pull out a handkerchief and wipe it across her eyes for fear that her tears would become far too overwhelming. Besides which, Laura would return with the maid very soon and it would not do for the girl to see her with red eyes and hear her hoarse voice.

And yet the words she had whispered echoed around the room, sending pain searing through her over and over again. She *was* lost. Set in an entirely new situation, without any real understanding of who and what she was now, Judith was left unsure of her own identity. Yes, she was a gentleman's daughter, but that did not carry any weight. Now, she was no longer to be in Lord Turton's company as someone who could dance in the same social sphere as he, but nor was she to be in the company of the staff. The loneliness was something she was used to, given that she had not had anyone to speak to, save for the infrequent company of her brother, for the last eighteen months, but there was another depth to this sense of isolation. It was, she realized, the understanding that there was no hope. That she was to be alone in the world in such a way for as long as her brother decreed it.

"Miss Newfield, the girl and I have returned."

Turning sharply, Judith frowned as the maid thrust the girl into the room with a little more force than was required.

"I must get back to my duties."

"Walking with Lady Laura in the grounds *is* one of your duties," Judith reminded her swiftly, as the maid's chin lifted, her eyes narrowing. "I shall expect you tomorrow, as usual." The maid opened her mouth to protest but Judith, anticipating this, spoke again. "I have already spoken to Lord Turton and expect to have a further conversation with him either today or tomorrow. If there is any concern on your part about whether or not you can fulfil your brief daily walk with Lady Laura, then pray do tell me now, so that I might bring it to him."

Shutting her mouth tightly, the maid turned around and marched out of the room, leaving the door to swing closed of its own accord. Giving a small smile towards the little girl, Judith walked back towards her desk, expecting the child to sit at her own also.

She did not.

Instead, little Laura dropped her head low, her shoulders slumping as her hands clasped lightly in front of her. Her dark hair, so similar in color to her father's, swung forward to shield her face.

Judith frowned, her own pain suddenly fading away in light of this small, crumpled child in front of her.

"Laura?" She did not give the girl her formal title, in the hope that there would be something of a kinship soon growing between them. "Are you quite well?"

I do not know why I ask her such things given that she will not speak.

Coming around her desk, she went to stand next to the girl, looking down at the dark head and finding herself quite at a loss.

"Do you not wish to do your letters today? I know it is a little difficult, but you did very well yesterday." Thus far, Judith had found Lady Laura to be an obedient, willing sort and, even though she had never said a single word these last few days, Judith had seen her begin her letters with evident earnestness. This strange unwillingness to even move from where she stood and go to sit down at her desk was very odd indeed and Judith was not certain how she ought to react.

A sniff caught her attention and instantly, Judith found herself crouching down, looking up into Laura's face. Was the girl crying?

"My dear child, whatever is the matter?" A ball of frustration formed within her as she fought hard to see what was troubling the girl. "I know that you will not speak to me as yet but might you show me? Is there a way that you can –"

Laura reached with one arm, twisting it over her other shoulder and rubbing at a spot on her back. Her light green eyes caught Judith's for just a second and Judith's heart ached at the tears which clung to the girl's lashes. Laura's hand moved again to her arm, rubbing at it hard.

Judith closed her eyes. She understood.

"You were hurt by the maid?" Reaching up, she gently rubbed the spot on Laura's back. "When she pushed you into the room?" Tears dripped onto Laura's cheeks, but she nodded, her face a little pale. "I am sorry about that. I will speak to her to make certain that she does not do so again." Making to get up, Judith's arm was caught by Laura's hand, and she gestured to her arm. Frowning, Judith stayed crouched down, trying to understand. "Your arm is sore also?" Seeing the child nod, Judith reached for it, wanting to have a look at the arm in question. Gently rolling up the sleeve, she gasped in shock at the light blue bruise which was already forming. "Did she pinch you?" The girl nodded. "Why?"

Laura blinked once, twice, and then one finger pointed to her mouth. She was shaking.

"To make you speak?" Anger began to boil in Judith's stomach, and she pressed her lips hard together in an attempt to hide her true reaction from the girl. "I am very sorry that such a thing happened, Laura. I will make sure that it does not occur again." Trying to smile, she pushed back Laura's dark hair over her ear. "You can trust me. I will make sure that you are not injured in such a way ever again."

The little girl's eyes stared back at her, unblinking, but

Judith merely smiled. Then, after some moments, the side of Laura's mouth twitched upwards and she blinked, before nodding her head.

"Good. You will not have to walk with that maid again. I promise you. I will take you out of doors myself if I must."

And I must speak with Lord Turton as soon as I can.

The little girl's smile grew, and, after a few moments, she walked to sit at her desk, her slate in front of her. Judith returned the smile as best she could, trying not to think of the bruise on the girl's arm, nor why the maid had thought to do such a thing. Mayhap the maid had become frustrated with Laura's silence, or mayhap she had thought to make the child speak so that she could find favor with Lord Turton, but either way, it was not at all acceptable. However, Judith could not simply abandon the child and go in search of her employer, demanding to speak to him, when his guests were already present. To do such a thing would only set her against him even more. Besides, she had now to concentrate solely on Laura, to help her continue with her education as best she could.

"I shall speak to your father today, Laura, I promise you."

Seeing the girl nod again, Judith let that promise rest on her heart, considering. Lord Turton might become angry with her, might be enraged that he had been so interrupted and indeed, might even question her responsibility and understanding of her station once again, but Judith was determined to keep her promise to Laura, no matter what faced her.

~

"I MUST SPEAK TO LORD TURTON."

The butler blinked in surprise, then shook his head.

"No, Miss Newfield. You cannot."

"I *must.*"

The butler again shook his head but this time, he drew himself up, standing as tall as he could so that he could look down at her.

"You may believe that you have cause to speak to the master, but I can assure you, it will not be of great enough importance for him to be interrupted."

"I believe that *I* am the only one able to be the judge of that." Lifting her chin and standing as tall as she could without raising her heels, Judith sent the butler a hard look. "You should not like to garner the master's displeasure, I hope?" The man blinked. "After all, given that I have a matter of importance regarding his daughter to bring to him, should it be delayed and I be asked why I hesitated in coming to speak with him, I should not like to have to state that it was his butler who detained me."

Again, the butler merely blinked back at her but rather than respond, he closed his eyes and let out a long, heavy sigh.

Now is the time for courage. The memory of Laura's pale, bruised arm returned to Judith's mind, and she steeled herself, pulling her hands tightly into fists.

"If you do not inform Lord Turton of my urgent request, then I shall have no other choice but to step into the dining room myself!"

"You cannot do such a thing, Miss Newfield!" the butler exclaimed at once, clearly horrified by the idea. "The master is sitting with the other gentleman, enjoying their port, and for you to even *consider* stepping into the room would be beyond all impropriety!"

Judith took a small step closer, tilting her head back a little more so that she could keep the butler's gaze.

"Then I suggest that you inform Lord Turton at an appropriate moment that I *must* speak with him and that I shall be waiting at his study. Else, I shall have no other choice but to interrupt him regardless of the circumstances."

So saying, she turned on her heel and marched down the hallway, praying silently that the butler would do as she asked. No doubt Lord Turton would be displeased with this interruption of his first night with his guests, but Judith was determined to keep her word. She could only hope that Lord Turton would take the matter as seriously as she.

"Miss Newfield!"

Judith started violently, her breath catching in a gasp as her fingers grasped the arms of the chair and her head swung wildly from one side to the other. Having found a chair by the window on the opposite side of the hallway from Lord Turton's study, she had sat down to rest as she waited and given her grogginess, had clearly fallen asleep.

"Whatever is the meaning of this?"

The sharp, angry words shot towards her as Judith rose unsteadily to her feet, blinking quickly so that her vision might focus itself a little better.

"Lord Turton, I –"

"I have already informed you once that you did not know your position as yet, but I had hoped that you would have taken such words into your heart, rather than dismiss them! You have no right to demand a meeting with me, regardless of how important your supposed issue is."

Still trying to gather herself together and finding herself wilting in the heat of Lord Turton's anger, Judith took in a deep breath and cleared her throat.

"Lord Turton, if you would –"

"I do not know why I am even *considering* keeping you in your position. After your display this afternoon in preventing me from meeting my guests at the appropriate time and now in interrupting my evening with my guests, I am not at all certain that you are the most appropriate person to be my daughter's governess!"

Judith took in another breath, ignoring the sting of his words against her skin.

"Lord Turton, it is because of your daughter that I have insisted upon this meeting."

"You can come to speak to me an appropriate time which, I am sure, my butler would be more than willing to inform you of, but to do so now –"

"If I might interrupt your tirade, Lord Turton, I am quite certain that it would save us both a lot of time."

Judith's heart thumped wildly in her chest as shock washed over her. She had not intended to speak in such a way and from the way Lord Turton's grey eyes widened, neither had he expected it of her.

"Miss Newfield." Lord Turton's voice was low, barely audible. "I –"

"One of your staff has deliberately been injuring your daughter." Judith spoke quickly, interrupting him again before he could think or say anything more. "I promised her that I would inform you of this before the day came to an end and I am a lady who keeps her word."

Lord Turton blinked rapidly, one hand running down over his face, pulling lightly at his chin.

"I–". Turning, he threw open the study door, all anger

and upset gone from his expression. "Come in, Miss Newfield. Please."

Relieved that he was not about to throw her from her position and his house at that very moment, even though she knew very well that she might deserve such a thing, given how she had spoken, Judith hurried into the study after Lord Turton. He took a few moments to light some additional candles, then turned back to face her.

"My daughter. What did she say to you?"

"She did not say anything, my Lord, for as yet, she still has not spoken."

"Then how did she make such a thing known to you?"

Taking in a deep breath, Judith explained about how the maid had pushed Laura into the room and how, thereafter, the child had refused to take her seat.

"When she gestured to her arm, I checked the skin and discovered a new and painful looking bruise. Your daughter confirmed through nods and glances that the maid had pinched her arm in an attempt to force her to speak." Lord Newfield looked away, a muscle in his jaw working furiously. "I promised your daughter that I would not have her go with that maid again, *and* that I would speak to you of the matter before the day was out. As I have said, my Lord, I am a lady who keeps my word and, whilst you will, no doubt, take umbrage with my insistence on seeing you this evening and on the sharpness of my words thereafter, I hope you can see that it was impossible for me to do otherwise."

Her explanation at an end, Judith linked her hands in front of her and looked up into Lord Turton's face, her stomach churning as icy fear began to pour through her veins. Fear that she would be dismissed from her position regardless, for even though her concern for Laura was well placed, she had spoken to Lord Turton in a most improper manner.

Lord Turton was still not looking at her. His head was turned away and his gaze fixed to a flickering candle to their right, but Judith watched the muscles in his jaw tighten and then relax over and over again. One glance at his hands told her than he was angry, for his hands were clenched into tight fists, his knuckles white.

"That maid will be dismissed from my staff." Lord Turton's voice was low and filled with a rage that Judith had never heard nor seen before and when he turned his head back to look at her, she shivered at the dark shadows in his eyes. "I will not abide someone treating my daughter so. I suppose she believed that Laura would never be able to say what had occurred and therefore did not hesitate. I–"

"I do not know the reason behind it, but you may well be correct, my Lord. It is good that Laura was willing to inform me of the truth."

A tiny flicker caught the edge of Lord Turton's lips.

"I suppose that is a small mercy, Miss Newfield."

Then he is not about to bring a swift end to my employment here.

Lord Turton swallowed, looking momentarily uncertain, then went on.

"I can see that there was a genuine urgency to your request to speak to me, Miss Newfield. I should have given your request a little more consideration, rather than immediately becoming frustrated by the interruption."

Judith held his gaze, licking her lips gently.

"I should not have been so outspoken, my Lord."

A dark chuckle broke from his lips.

"You are not the most conventional of governesses, Miss Newfield. However, I shall say that you have proven that this unconventionality is greatly beneficial and for good purpose in this regard, at least." His small smile faded. "Please reassure my daughter that she has nothing to fear. This maid will never again be in her company."

"Thank you, Lord Turton. There is more that I wish to discuss with you about your daughter, but nothing so pressing nor urgent. At a more convenient time, perhaps. As I have said, I am grateful to you for permitting me to speak at this present moment."

Shaking his head, he suddenly rested one hand lightly on her shoulder, and Judith was caught by surprise at the gentleness in his expression. The dark shadows in his eyes had faded and his jaw was no longer tight. Instead, his eyes met hers, and his mouth was soft, although he did not smile.

"No, Miss Newfield. It is I who is most grateful to you." His fingers pressed her shoulder gently and Judith's heart suddenly quickened. "I will deal with this matter at once."

She nodded, strangely eager to linger in his presence now.

"Thank you, Lord Turton. I should return to Laura, to make certain that she is asleep and resting. Good evening."

His hand lifted and the warmth which had been building in her heart quickly faded as he nodded.

"Good evening, Miss Newfield. And thank you."

CHAPTER FIVE

"She is dismissed, then?"

The butler nodded.

"Yes, my Lord."

"Perhaps I ought not to have been so willing to give her references," David muttered, passing one hand over his eyes and leaning back in his chair.

"I am certain that she was more than grateful for them, my Lord." The butler shook his head to himself. "I did not know that she had been injuring Lady Laura so. I can only apologize for–"

"No need for apology, Burch. It was not something that you could easily have been aware of. Not something that any of us would have been aware of, had it not been for Miss Newfield." A flicker of warmth struck his heart and David allowed his mouth to curve into a small smile. "I am grateful to her and for her insistence on interrupting me last evening."

The butler closed his eyes briefly.

"I am relieved to hear that, my Lord."

"Indeed, she is somewhat unconventional but, in this

regard, at least, has proven her worth." Clearing his throat and trying to push away all thought of Miss Newfield for the time being, David sat straighter in his chair and picked up the first of his correspondence. "That is all, Burch. Pray do inform me when my guests have risen."

"But of course."

Bowing, the butler took himself from the study and left David alone with his thoughts – thoughts which came thick and fast.

Miss Newfield.

The way she had spoken to him last night had been more than a little improper, given her station, and her sharp tongue had left him quite astonished, but now that he looked back upon the matter, David found himself more than a little appreciative of such traits. Had she not done so, then he could have easily dismissed her request continually – something, he realized, he had already been doing.

Closing his eyes, David scowled to himself. He had pushed Miss Newfield away some three times already, he was sure. Last evening, she had asked for another opportunity, soon, to speak with him about his daughter and rather than ignore such a request, David was determined to make certain that they spoke together very soon. He owed her that, at least.

Miss Newfield is the most extraordinary creature of my acquaintance.

"She ought not to be a governess," he muttered to himself, breaking the seal of his first letter. "She ought to be preparing for the London Season, ready to make a match with whichever fortunate gentleman might wish to marry her."

"Did I hear you speak of matrimony?"

David started violently, half rising out of his chair

before he realized that it was none other than Lady Madeline who had come into his study. She was dressed in a light blue gown, with her hair neatly coiled and pulled back from her face, although delicate, gentle wisps of gold brushed at her temples. Her beautiful blue eyes, framed with thick, dark lashes, twinkled at him and her rosebud lips curved into a teasing smile.

David did not return it.

"Lady Madeline, whatever are you doing here?"

"I came to speak with you."

Blinking in surprise, he shook his head.

"You cannot. You have no chaperone."

She closed the door behind her, showing more determination than he had ever seen in her before.

"I do not think that I require a chaperone if I am simply visiting my betrothed." Tilting her head, she wandered slowly towards him, but David's concern only grew. "My mother is still involved in her preparations for the day and thus, you find me rather bored. I did not want to sit and wait, so I thought instead that I might come and speak with you for some minutes." She laughed, but the soft, tinkling sound scraped hard, setting David's teeth on edge. "After all, what can be done if someone discovers us? It is not as though we are not already betrothed."

"That is true, certainly."

Rising from his chair, David did not make his way around the desk towards his betrothed, choosing instead to keep the large desk between them. Strangely enough, he had no desire to take her into his arms nor to permit himself the opportunity to kiss her, despite her incredible beauty. Whenever he looked at her, David found himself lost in worry, afraid that their betrothal had been too hasty and that he was now bound to a creature whom he knew very little about.

All the more reason, then, to make endeavors to know her character a little better.

"I do not think this wise, however." Trying to soften his words with a smile, David shrugged. "I should not like to upset your mother in any way."

Lady Madeline trilled a laugh.

"You need not worry about such a thing, Lord Turton," she said, dismissively. "My mother is much too caught up in her own particular enhancements and will have not a single thought about where I have gone, I assure you."

This did not give David any comfort whatsoever.

"All the same, Lady Madeline, I do not wish to behave with any impropriety."

"Impropriety?" Her eyebrows lifted, then settled into a gentle frown. "My dear Lord Turton, we are betrothed! We are soon to be wed, are we not? What impropriety can there be between us when we are to become husband and wife?"

Those words sent a chill through David's heart, but he did his utmost to ignore them, instead doing his best to smile at Lady Madeline so that the frown she wore would not linger.

"You are correct, of course, but I should much rather be cautious, Lady Madeline. There are many delights to come, and to hasten them would not be of any worth."

Rather than permit the desk to remain between them, Lady Madeline began to make her way around towards him, leaving David with no choice other than to turn to face her. It was not as though he could back away, for that would bring her great upset, which was precisely the very thing that David wanted to avoid. And yet, he did not want to draw close to her, did not want to make the most of a few minutes alone with the lady. Looking into her face and reminding himself of just how beautiful a creature she was, David waited for his heart to begin to yearn for her, for his desire to begin to grow so that he could do nothing *but* pull her close – but it did not come.

"There are *some* delights that I am certain we need not wait for, Turton." Lady Madeline's voice was soft, her eyes holding a spark that David himself did not share. "You have been every inch the gentleman – aside from the fact that you did not seek my father's permission before you proposed – and I cannot help but think that you have been patient enough." One hand caught his wrist, her fingers then brushing lightly up his arm towards his shoulder – but David felt no heat spiral in his chest. Instead, his skin prickled uncomfortably, and he had to force himself to remain standing exactly where he was, rather than pull himself back from her.

"I know that *I* have been patient enough."

"You quite astonish me, Lady Madeline." David spoke with honesty, and his betrothed merely laughed, his eyes sparkling as her lips pulled into a smile. "I did not think that you would ever seek such a thing, or behave in this particularly overt manner."

Her smile did not fade.

"There is a good deal you do not know of me yet, it seems."

And that is of great concern to me.

"It seems that is so, Lady Madeline." Clearing his throat as her fingers brushed the skin at the nape of his neck, David did not lift his hand. "But all the same, I must stand by my principles."

Looking into her eyes, he saw the light fade from them, her smile shattering slowly.

"I see." Her hand dropped from his shoulder and a small sigh emitted from her lips. "You are a gentleman of great determination, it seems."

"I am, certainly."

"And I do not think that I should hold such a thing against you, even though I have taken great pains to arrive at your study without being seen so that we might have a few minutes alone together."

Her fingers caught his, twining through them, and David forced a smile – one which he hoped was a little regretful.

"Alas, I must be a gentleman of principle, still, despite your great efforts. Forgive me, Lady Madeline. I do hope that I have not injured your feelings in any way."

She sighed and stepped back, allowing a breath of relief to escape carefully from David's lips.

"Alas, I am a little injured, but I shall not permit it to cause me any great pain, given that it has been done so chivalrously." Her smile returned but it was somewhat dimmed. "I must hope that you do not think ill of me for my... forwardness."

A slight pink hue came to her cheeks and David quickly sought to reassure her.

"Not in the least, Lady Madeline." Smiling, he gave her a half bow. "I appreciate your understanding. I am a gentleman to the core."

"Indeed, for I have never heard it suggested that there is even the smallest hint of rakishness in you." A small twist of Lady Madeline's lips caught David's attention and he frowned, wondering if she somehow thought less of him because of this. "I should return to my room now. My mother will wish us to walk to the dining room together so that we might break our fast."

"I will join you in a few minutes," he told her, more than a little relieved when she stepped out of the room.

The door closed softly, and David sank down into his chair, putting his head in his hands and resting his elbows on the desk in front of him.

What am I going to do?

David had never declared – neither to himself nor to any other – that he would make a love match, should he marry again, for indeed, his first marriage had been one of arrangement, although that in itself had turned out to be a deeply unhappy situation. Now, however, to find himself no longer *drawn* to Lady Madeline was most disconcerting. Yes, there was still some impropriety in her being in company with him without a chaperone, but not everyone would frown upon it, given that they were betrothed. Her desire to be physically close to him had been more than apparent but, recalling his own lack of eagerness, David groaned aloud, squeezing his eyes closed tightly.

"I was overcome by her beauty and acted foolishly." Muttering to himself, he shoved one hand through his hair and dropped the other to the desk. "And now I am betrothed. To a lady whom I find not even the smallest desire for within my heart."

~

"Good morning, Lady Heslington, Lady Madeline." Relieved that there were more than just these two ladies sitting at the dining table, David greeted the others also. "Lady Richardson, Lady Juliet, Lord Gregory." Turning at the sound of the door opening, he grinned at Lord Carr, who was still looking rather weary. "And Lord Carr. Good morning to you all."

His other guests all smiled and nodded and sent words of greeting towards him, whilst Lady Madeline merely blushed, dropped her gaze, and hid a smile. David noticed how Lady Juliet leaned towards her, whispering something which made Lady Madeline giggle.

Just what has she told her friend?

"It is a very fine day, is it not?" Lord Gregory said, waving one hand towards the window. "A *very* fine day indeed! Perhaps a fine day for shooting?"

"Oh, I should dislike it *very* much if the gentlemen went shooting and left the ladies behind," Lady Madeline protested immediately, pouting in a somewhat childish manner. "We have only a few days with Lord Turton and to deprive us of your company so that you might go shooting would be most disagreeable. No, I do not think that shooting would be at all the thing to do."

Folding her hands in her lap, she looked up at David and smiled, seemingly content in *her* determination and fully expecting him to agree with her.

David chewed his lip, glancing back at Lord Gregory. Whilst Lady Madeline was free to express her opinion, he did not much like that she pouted in such a fashion, nor that she declared in such a manner that *she* ought to have what she wanted – namely, none of the gentlemen absent from her day. That indicated a lack of consideration that David did not appreciate and, as such, he found himself speaking in direct contradiction.

"I say that the day is a fine day for shooting, yes. I could have everything arranged for the afternoon?" Glancing at Lady Madeline, he saw her frown, her light blue eyes suddenly dark. "That way, the ladies can enjoy our company this morning for a short while before we step out to shoot. I am certain that there can be no real disagreement about such an arrangement. This evening, of course, we will dine together and thereafter, I have the most excellent entertainment for us all."

This brought smiles to everyone's faces, save for that of Lady Madeline, who continued to pout and look away.

"I fear that you will displease your betrothed if you continue with this endeavor," Lord Carr murmured, as he passed David to make his way to a seat.

David shrugged inwardly but threw Lord Carr a wry smile.

"If the ladies would wish to, I could arrange for a carriage to take you to the nearest village, or simply to enjoy a drive? There are a few shops which might be of interest."

"How adorably quaint they must be," Lady Richardson exclaimed, as her daughter smiled and nodded. "I think that an excellent idea, Lord Turton. I thank you for your consideration."

"Then it is settled! I shall make certain that all of the arrangements are made for both parties so that we might enjoy the day immensely."

The group quickly fell into conversation, leaving David to fill his plate and then make his way to the table. A seat next to Lady Madeline was vacant, but just as David began to make his way there – feeling obliged to do so rather than having any genuine willingness – Lord Gregory sat down next to her and began conversing at once. A little relieved, David watched as Lady Madeline's pout faded, although she still did not smile. Leaning a little closer to Lord Gregory, she began to talk rather quickly, whilst Lord Gregory nodded in evident understanding.

If he manages to pull her out of this dark mood, then I shall be forever in his debt.

Grimacing, David made his way to another seat and sat

down beside his friend, rolling his eyes as Lord Carr arched one eyebrow and tilted his head in Lady Madeline's direction.

"I did not expect her to be so upset," David said, by way of explanation. "It was not deliberately to frustrate her but rather to do what I think would be most beneficial for my guests."

Lord Carr shot another look towards Lady Madeline.

"I am not certain that she will understand that."

"I was unaware that Lady Madeline had such a stubbornness about her."

"She is merely sharing what it is that *she* thinks would be best, that is all," came the response. "I doubt that anyone, gentleman *or* lady would be contented with being so overruled."

"But it is my house, and this is my house party." Screwing up his face, David shook his head. "Forgive me. That makes me sound like a petulant child."

"It does, rather," Lord Carr answered. "But I understand your frustration. It may be that your lingering frustration over the governess has seeped into this day also and you find yourself now to be a little overwhelmed."

David frowned.

"The governess?" Lord Carr nodded, before lifting some food to his mouth. "Ah, yes." David recalled that he had spoken briefly to Lord Carr after he had been informed by the butler that the governess was insisting upon seeing him. Lord Carr had led the rest of the gentlemen to the drawing-room whilst David had made his way to his study. "That was certainly somewhat infuriating, until I realized that she had called me for a very specific purpose with regard to my daughter. I cannot confess to being frustrated now."

"I see."

Lord Carr's brow lifted but he did not ask any further questions, leaving David to ruminate.

The truth was, both Lady Madeline and Miss Newfield expressed the same strong, determined attitude but, whilst David had found both frustrating in their own way, he recognized now that Miss Newfield's determination had come solely from her concern for his daughter, whereas Lady Madeline's declarations had been only about her and her preferences. They could not be held up in the same light.

"You still have doubts about your future with the lady."

Snapping out of his reverie, David turned to Lord Carr, grateful that he had spoken quietly.

"I confess that I do." Keeping his voice low, he allowed himself to speak honestly. "This has only confirmed to me that I do not know Lady Madeline particularly well at all, and I am afraid that, the more I discover of her character, the more I will regret our betrothal."

"Then mayhap you should seek a way to remove the betrothal in such a manner that it brings very little difficulty to you both, should such a circumstance occur. I know that you are a gentleman of honor, and that you are inclined simply to step forward and hold to the decision which you have made, but I would encourage you to think again. There must be something you can do which would bring the betrothal to a close without causing any great scandal."

David shook his head, but his thoughts twisted at his immediate refusal.

"I am not certain that I could do such a thing. I have offered her my hand and she has accepted. To break us apart now, simply because I was a fool in rushing forward, would be unfair to her."

"Then consider this, my dear friend. Consider your future. Consider what your life will be like, should you step into a marriage that you know will not please you. Is it fair to the lady, *and* to yourself, that you push forward to a future which will bring you both a great deal of unhappiness?" Opening his mouth to respond, David found that there were no words on his lips. Frowning hard, he shook his head again but did not say anything further. "Think on it, Turton. The last thing I should like to see is you wed and facing a future of both unhappiness and regret. It would not be fair for either of you."

Taking a deep breath, David let his gaze linger on Lady Madeline. She was smiling now, looking up at Lord Gregory as he grinned back at her, talking and gesticulating about some matter or other. There was so much beauty in her outward appearance but still, David was not certain that her character was equally beautiful. Perhaps what Lord Carr had said ought to be considered. After all, any future which brought them *both* despondence would be nothing but difficulty and he would do well to consider that.

"I shall think on what you have said."

Lord Carr smiled, but the concern in his eyes did not fade.

"I am glad to hear it."

"And now I must go to arrange the shooting." Pushing his chair back, David rose and made to excuse himself. "Thank you, Carr. That was an enlightening conversation."

With a nod, his friend returned to his breakfast whilst David made his way to the door. Glancing at Lady Madeline and expecting her to be already looking at him, David was a little surprised when he saw that she was still much too taken up with all that Lord Gregory had to say. He had thought that she would be watching *him*, wanting to know where he was going and, mayhap, making it expressly clear that she was displeased with his departure.

Her eyes suddenly caught his and David smiled, only for Lady Madeline to look away again. As David watched, her hand reached out and touched Lord Gregory's arm – but only for a moment.

Anger began to build in David's chest, and he turned away, pulling open the door and stepping out into the hallway.

She is goading me.

Closing the door tightly behind him, David strode down the hallway towards his study, his hands balling into fists. Lady Madeline, upset with his decision to go ahead with the shooting even though *she* did not wish it, had decided that she would make her point by ignoring him *and* by being a little flirtatious with Lord Gregory. Was she attempting to make him jealous? Trying to force him into retracting his plans to give way to hers?

"I have no intention of doing so." His words bounced down the hallway and back towards him, his voice overly loud due to his growing anger. Suddenly the idea of finding a way to break the betrothal without causing a scandal seemed to be a very good idea indeed, and David silently determined that he would begin to consider what he might do over the next few days. Instead of making wedding plans, he would seek a way to withdraw his connection to Lady Madeline altogether, otherwise, David feared, his future would look very dark indeed.

CHAPTER SIX

"Would you like to take a walk?"

The way that Laura's eyes flared wide as the color drained from her cheeks made Judith realize instantly that she had made a mistake.

"I do not mean with the maid," she clarified quickly, coming across to the little girl and bending down to look directly into her face. "I must apologize to you, my dear child. I quite forgot to tell you that I had spoken with your father last evening, as I said I would." Laura's wide eyes searched her face and Judith smiled, reaching out to squeeze the little girl's hand. "He stated that the maid would not be allowed to walk with you again. Indeed, I believe that he has dismissed her from her position." Seeing Laura bite her lip, Judith took the girl's other hand also, wanting to reassure her still further. "You will never see her again and should anything like that ever happen to you again – although I would be very surprised if it did – I should like you to tell me in whatever way you can." Smiling, she tilted her head. "Do you think that you can do that?"

After a few moments, Laura nodded slowly.

"Very good. Now, if you wish to go for a walk, I should be glad to join you. We could walk together!" Thus far, Lord Turton had not thought to provide Judith with another maid to take Laura out of doors for a short while in the afternoon – something she had been granted since her arrival – and thus, there was nothing for Judith to do but to take the child out of doors herself. To her surprise, she did not feel any frustration or irritation at such a thing but was, instead, rather relieved that she was able to stay by the girl's side. There was something of a protectiveness in her heart now which, whilst a surprising emotion was not something that Judith balked at. "Would you like that? If we were to walk together out of doors?"

"Yes."

Judith blinked in utter astonishment, only for Laura to put one finger in her mouth and then turn away towards the door, clearly ready to step out of doors. Judith pushed herself slowly up to standing, her heart beating with a sudden great and wild relief, questioning silently whether or not she had truly heard the child speak.

I must not react in an overt fashion.

Judith went to stand beside Laura, and then, holding one hand out to her, smiled brightly, praying that this one word would soon be the start of many more.

"Come, then."

The little girl's hand curled into hers and Judith's smile only grew, her heart still beating with such a furious rhythm that she wanted to laugh aloud for the sheer joy of it. She was quite sure that Laura had said something to her – albeit it in a whispered voice – and that single word had brought such a fierce joy to Judith's heart that she could barely contain it. But contain it she must, for a loud, overt reaction might very easily scare the child into complete silence once again. *Should I tell Lord Turton?*

Judith considered, tilting her head towards Laura as she walked to the front of the house. From what she knew of him, Lord Turton was a man of quick reactions. Slow to consider what the situation might be rather than what he immediately thought of it, he might very well race up to the schoolroom and demand that Laura say something to him, should she tell him of what had occurred. No, she determined, it would be best, for the moment, to remain silent on the matter and wait until Laura herself wished to speak to her father. The child was old enough to make that particular decision alone.

I do wonder why she has not spoken to Lord Turton since her arrival here, Judith considered, as they stepped out into the glorious afternoon sunshine which made the autumnal day so very beautiful and warm. *It was a strange circumstance that he described to me – his wife and daughter living in an entirely different house from him? Why would he make such an arrangement?*

"Shall we make our way to the pond and see if there is anything interesting there?" Judith smiled as Laura nodded eagerly, her finger no longer at her mouth and a bright smile spreading across her face. "I have heard that your father and his gentlemen guests are shooting today so we cannot stray too close to the nearby woods."

Laura did not seem to mind for she let go of Judith's hand and began to run towards the pond, leaving Judith to shout a warning to be careful and to quicken her steps after her. The child threw up her arms and spun around, making her delight at being out of doors obvious to everyone who could see her. Judith smiled, noticing even the gardener lifting his head to watch Laura dance across the grass towards the pond.

And then, Laura stopped. Her arms fell to her sides, and she came to an absolute standstill. With the pond in view, Judith walked quickly towards her, putting one arm around her shoulders.

"Laura? Are you quite all right?"

The girl glanced up at her, then pointed straight ahead. Looking at the pond, Judith frowned, unable to see anything strange or out of place. And then, something caught her attention, and she lifted her gaze slightly, seeing something moving in the trees just beyond.

Her chest tightened as a flurry of nervousness ran through her veins.

"I am sure it is just the wind," she said, speaking with as much confidence as she could. "Come now, I am sure we will see the little fish in the pond if we are quiet. The sunshine is so very warm."

Laura looked up at her, considering. Then she nodded and walked towards the pond, leaving Judith to follow after.

Licking her lips, Judith clasped her hands tightly in front of her and walked to the pond, keeping her gaze focused on the trees. There had been something, or someone, in amongst that small copse of trees, she was sure of it. Laura's hand caught hers and Judith held it tightly, glancing behind her to make sure that the gardener was still present. At least they were not out here alone.

Laura tugged on her hand and Judith was forced to drop her attention back to the pond rather than gaze at the trees. Laura pointed eagerly at the little fish swimming in amongst the reeds and Judith smiled, her worry fading away. Together, she and Laura began to count how many fish there were, with Judith speaking aloud and Laura counting silently on her fingers. An idea caught in her mind and Judith smiled.

"So, there are nine fish?"

Laura shook her head, holding up both hands, fingers, and thumbs spread wide.

"Nine."

Again, the little girl shook her head.

"I am sure there were only nine." Shaking her head, Judith looked back at the pond rather than at the girl's hands. "Mayhap we should count again."

Laura grabbed Judith's arm, making her turn back to face her.

"Ten."

The whisper was barely there but it was loud enough to hear. Laura's face was pinched, as though she knew exactly what Judith had been trying to do and was frustrated that she had given in. But regardless, Judith felt a swell of delight in her heart, bending down to look into Laura's face, her hand pushing back her dark hair behind her ear.

"Yes, there are ten." Smiling softly, she waited until Laura eventually smiled back, her eyes darting away, looking a little abashed. "You did very well, my dear girl. I am very proud of you."

Laura smiled and then slipped her hand back into Judith's.

"Perhaps a walk to the rose garden? The gardener has been pruning them and there are still some beautiful blooms."

Nodding, Judith turned and led Laura away from the pond, her heart full of happiness and relief. Another whispered word from Laura had filled her heart and left her with such gladness that she could barely contain it. Throwing a quick glance behind her back towards the pond,

Judith's breath hitched, her smile fading. Something was moving through the trees once more – nothing more than a vague shadow, but still present, nonetheless. Laura slipped her hand from hers and ran forward towards the rose garden, not noticing, but Judith remained where she was. The figure moved again and this time, Judith made the person out clearly. She saw him moving quickly through the edge of the trees, making little attempt now to hide. Had he realized she had seen him?

Turning on her heel, Judith hurried towards the gardener, who was now busy talking to Laura. Forcing a false smile, Judith patted Laura on the shoulder and the girl looked up.

"Why don't you see if you can find me the prettiest bloom?"

Laura smiled, her eyes bright before she turned and scurried away through the rose garden. Judith wasted no time, turning to the gardener.

"There is someone in the trees." Pointing to the pond, she saw him glance back at it. "I am certain I saw a figure in amongst them."

The gardener nodded slowly, appearing not to be at all perturbed.

"Yes, Miss Newfield. There might very well be."

Her racing heart began to slow.

"You are aware of such a person?"

Shrugging, the gardener spread his hands.

"There will be plenty of them out today, Miss Newfield, what with the shooting."

A frown pulled at her brow.

"I do not understand."

"There are a few young lads from the village who poach on the master's lands sometimes." The gardener shrugged.

"They'll be trying to steal a pheasant or two from under their noses." He did not smile nor frown but rather spoke with a great deal of calm, as though this was something to be expected. "The groundskeeper has one or two men out with him, keeping an eye on things. It is probably one of them that you saw." Evidently seeing fright in her expression, he smiled kindly, his eyes gentle. "Don't worry, Miss Newfield. I'm sorry if you were frightened."

A long, slow breath escaped her, and Judith closed her eyes, then opened them again, finding herself smiling when she looked back at him.

"Thank you. That makes me feel a good deal better."

"Of course, Miss Newfield."

Looking over to where Laura was jumping up and down and pointing at a rose, Judith smiled and let her shoulders drop, feeling the tension flood away from her.

"I should go to Laura. Thank you again."

Walking towards her charge, Judith could not help but throw another glance over her shoulder, back towards the pond. There was nothing there, no movement or person to be seen, and Judith shook her head to herself, telling herself silently that she was being quite ridiculous.

Even if there had been someone, it was someone who was meant to be present, meant to be on the premises. There was nothing to concern her, nothing to worry at her mind. Her only responsibility now was to Laura and, recalling the two words that the child had spoken today, Judith found her heart lifting with a fresh and exciting hope that Laura might, one day, be able to speak openly with her and, thereafter, with Lord Turton. She could only pray that it would be soon.

~

"Lady Laura is already asleep, Miss Newfield."

Judith looked up from where she had been attempting to read a book, albeit with eyes that were heavy with sleep.

"Oh. I see." She smiled at the maid and, after a moment, the girl smiled back. She had not often been in the schoolroom with Judith and Laura, but after the previous maid had been dismissed, Judith assumed that this maid had been sent to take her place. "Thank you. What is your name, might I ask?"

"Christie."

"And have you worked long for Lord Turton?"

"A few years, yes." The maid leaned against the doorframe of the schoolroom, clearly unwilling to return to her duties below stairs. "I came before Lady Turton was sent away."

Judith nodded slowly, her breath hitching, although the maid did not seem to notice. This was evidently something which was well known amongst the staff.

"Might I ask you something about Lady Turton?"

The maid nodded.

"Of course."

"I do not know the circumstances surrounding her removal to another house. It seems rather strange to me that a husband would encourage such a thing, and I should say that I personally think that the situation thereafter seems to have injured Lady Laura somewhat, given her silence."

The maid nodded.

"I think it must have done. I didn't work in the house, but I know that Lady Laura talked a lot when she lived with her mother, and even after the poor lady died."

Judith's heart twisted at the thought of Laura losing one of her parents and being left in a house with only the servants to care for her.

"I assume, then, that Laura did not know much of Lord Turton."

"No, I don't think she did. Lord Turton didn't go to visit them very often, from what I know. And they were never allowed back here."

Curiosity pricked Judith's mind.

"Why was she sent away? What was it that had happened?" Seeing the maid look away, she spoke quickly. "I do not mean to pry, but Lord Turton has said nothing about it and I should like to know, for Laura's sake alone. It may be that something about that situation has caused her now to fall silent and if I can –"

"Lord Turton would not tell you the truth, even if you asked him," the maid interrupted, scowling as she looked away. "It wasn't a love match. Lady Turton – her father – wanted her to marry well, and Lord Turton needed a bride. I don't think they ever actually cared for each other."

Judith nodded.

"I can understand the situation." It was something which took place very often, although Judith herself had not wanted to consider such a thing. "They married, Laura was born and then she was removed to another house?"

"Oh, no, that is not what happened." The maid leaned forward, her voice dropping low as if she wanted to keep the truth a secret. "Lady Turton was sent away *before* Laura was born. It was well known that she was with child, however, and some of us thought that the master simply wanted her to have a quiet place to recover and rest. But when the baby was born, he did not go to see her, or the baby, for some weeks! And thereafter, it became quite clear that the master had no intention of Lady Turton and the baby ever returning to this house."

"I see." A dark idea flickered in Judith's mind, but she

did not permit it to take hold. "And then Lady Turton became ill?"

The maid nodded.

"The physicians were sent for, but there was nothing that could be done for her. From what I was told, it happened very quickly. And then we all thought that the child would come here to reside with her father, but he left her there, back at that house with only the staff to look after her."

"You can't think that was the right thing to do." Judith's lips twisted and she looked away. "I know that I do not."

Shrugging, Christie sighed.

"It don't matter what we think. But yes, Miss Newfield, I think that Laura would have been better here. That they *both* would have been better here. But Lord Turton had his reasons, even if we don't really know what they are."

"But you can guess." The flash in the maid's eyes told Judith that she had the very same thoughts as Judith did. "That would explain a great deal, I suppose," she murmured, half to herself. "If it were to be true."

"But we shan't know, so it is not worth thinking about," Christie replied, the firmness in her voice telling Judith that this was something which had been discussed before by the servants but where they had then been very firmly told not to talk about the matter anymore. "All that matters is that Laura is here and that we take the very best care of her we can."

Judith smiled.

"Of course. Thank you for talking with me, Christie. It has been.... difficult to know what to think when it comes to how Laura has been treated."

The maid smiled, nodded, and bade Judith good night, before stepping out of the schoolroom and leaving Judith alone with her thoughts. Judith tried to turn back to her book, to prepare herself for what she was to do with Laura tomorrow, but found that she simply could not concentrate.

Did Lord Turton discover that Laura was not his daughter?

That seemed to be the most obvious explanation, for what gentleman would send his wife and unborn child away to reside elsewhere? Why would he refuse to visit, refuse to acknowledge the birth until some weeks later? It all seemed very odd indeed, and yet the only explanation which made sense was that Lord Turton feared that Laura was not legitimate.

Not that it will make any difference to how I treat the girl. Smiling to herself, Judith rose from her chair and walked to the window, shaking her head to herself. Regardless of whether Lady Laura was, or was not, the daughter of Lord Turton, Judith was becoming slowly more protective and concerned for her. She already cared for the girl a great deal, which was far more than she had ever expected.

"Perhaps I am well suited to being a governess."

Wrapping her arms about her waist, Judith looked out across the gardens in the dim, fading evening light. The last few golden rays of the low autumnal sun spread across the grounds and made Judith's heart lift with the sheer beauty of it. It was strange just how much contentment she felt at present, standing here in the schoolroom, dressed in her drab governess' gown. Her life had changed in a thousand different ways and yet she had found a sense of relief, and even enjoyment, in these last two days. In finding a resolve with Lord Turton and now hearing Laura speak to her, Judith was beginning to find herself settled in this new situation, albeit with a lingering sense of loss over her status as a lady of society. A laugh escaped her as she thought about just how easily she had spoken with a maid – something she would never really have done had she been at home with her brother.

Sighing to herself, Judith dropped her hands and was about to make her way back to her desk when she noticed something catch her eye. Frowning, she gazed down at the grounds and, much to her astonishment, noticed someone walking across the grass. Her eyes narrowed as she fixed her gaze on them, seeing their head turn this way and that, as though they were looking furtively all about to make certain that they were not seen. Their shoulders were pulled in, their frame hunched, and their steps quick and hasty.

Something is wrong.

Judith's stomach twisted as the figure made their way towards the house, continually looking over their shoulder. Biting her lip, she considered whether or not she ought to go to tell Lord Turton of what she had seen, only to then recall the gardener's words to her.

It is either someone that is stealing from Lord Turton and ought not to be, else it is someone that Lord Turton is already acquainted with, who has come to visit. I may think that he appears furtive, but that might well be my own misapprehension. Biting her lip, Judith forced herself to turn away. *Although it is strange that he does not come on horseback or by carriage if he is come to call.*

"Enough." Speaking aloud, Judith made her way to her desk and sat down with a sigh. She was not about to embarrass herself in front of Lord Turton by going to tell him that she had seen someone in the garden. Even as she thought about it, she saw his grey eyes turning to dark slate and his lips pulling taut and felt her cheeks burn. No, she would not speak to him, not yet. He had still to grant her an opportunity to speak with him at length about Laura and given that such a thing had not yet taken place, Judith did not think it would be wise to interrupt him about such a small matter as this. No doubt he would think her foolish and that was the last thing she wanted.

To her surprise, Judith found that her thoughts did not want to depart from Lord Turton. Instead, she caught herself thinking of his eyes, his lips, his broad shoulders, and the strength that he carried in his frame. Unbidden, she recalled how they had stood close together at the top of the stairs, remembering the heat of his breath on her cheek, the way his dark hair had brushed across his forehead as he had lowered his head to speak quietly to her. She had felt all manner of clamoring emotions at that juncture, but she had never once thought herself caught by the gentleman's appearance!

And then you saw him walking with Lady Madeline and your heart ached with such a pain that tears came to your eyes.

"That is only because I felt myself so much lesser than I have ever been before," Judith said aloud, determined not to give in to any thought to the contrary. "It was not at all because Lady Madeline was on Lord Turton's arm. That is ridiculous. Entirely ridiculous."

But try as she might, the notion that it might have had a little to do with Lady Madeline's closeness to Lord Turton would not leave her, no matter how hard she tried to push it away. Confused and frustrated with her own lack of strength, Judith rose from her desk and went to collect Laura's slate. She could not permit herself to think this way, for that would, she knew, only lead to difficulty and uncertainty which would, in the end, lead to nothing but trouble and mortification on her part – and that was something which Judith was quite determined to avoid.

CHAPTER SEVEN

"My Lord?"

David looked up from his correspondence.

"Yes?"

The butler cleared his throat.

"The gardener wishes to speak to you, my Lord. On an urgent matter."

Blinking away his surprise, David nodded and gestured for the man to come in. Stepping aside, the butler made way for the gardener who came in on shuffling feet, his cap twisting in his hands.

"My Lord." He bowed his head, his eyes looking anywhere but into David's face. "I'm sorry to interrupt you, but something happened yesterday that I thought it best to tell you about. I know that you have house guests and I–"

"That is of no importance. Whatever you have to say, I am ready and willing to hear."

The gardener finally looked at him, nodded and then cleared his throat.

"My Lord, when you were out shooting yesterday afternoon, Miss Newfield and Lady Laura were out in the garden."

Alarm suddenly shot through David, and he sat up a little straighter.

"There was not an accident?"

Had Miss Newfield not come to tell him out of fear that he would react with such fury that she would be gone from his house? Was Laura hurt? The thought of his daughter lying injured on a bed somewhere in the house whilst he enjoyed an evening's soiree had his breathing becoming suddenly labored.

"No, my Lord, there was no accident or injury. Both Miss Newfield and Lady Laura were quite well. They went back to the house after a walk in the rose garden."

"Oh." Sinking back into his chair, David let out a long breath of relief. "I apologize for the interruption."

Waving a hand, he gestured for the man to continue.

"Before the rose garden, Lady Laura wanted to go to the pond. Miss Newfield was with her. When she came to speak to me – with Lady Laura looking at the roses, Miss Newfield told me that she had seen someone in the trees."

Every single muscle in David's body tensed at once, his jaw tightening as he looked back at the gardener and saw the heaviness in his expression.

"You mean to say that you think someone was spying on this house?"

"I don't know, my Lord. But given what you struggled against in the past, I thought it was best to inform you."

David closed his eyes, a sudden weight resting on his shoulders.

"That was a wise consideration." Leaning forward, he set one elbow on the desk and let his fingers push through his hair. "I had thought that, with my wife's passing, the matter would have come to an end." The gardener said nothing, his large hands twisting his cap back and forth in his hands. "It has been *years* since the last time." Looking up at the man, David held his gaze. "Is that not so?"

"I believe you are right, my Lord. Once you sent Lady Turton from the house, the threat began to fade."

"But now it might have returned. I do not know why that could be but –"

"If I may, my Lord?" The gardener chewed his lip and David looked back at him, nodding his encouragement. "It may be that news of your daughter has spread through England, since she has come to live here now. Perhaps it wasn't known before that Lady Turton had a daughter."

Something heavy dropped into the pit of David's stomach and he nodded.

"That is again, a wise thought. I appreciate your loyalty and your wisdom a great deal. There will be an additional bonus in your wages this month."

Rather than smile, the gardener dropped his head.

"I didn't come to tell you in the hope of more money, my Lord."

"I know you did not." Rising, David walked around his desk and gripped the gardener's hand, in such a way as he might do with a gentleman acquaintance. "But your loyalty to myself, to my late wife, and now to my daughter is noted and will be rewarded."

The gardener shook his hand briefly, then dropped his hand back to his side.

"If there is anything else I can do, my Lord?"

"Nothing but keep watching, as you have been already." Making his way back to his desk, David stopped suddenly and spun on his heel. "Wait a moment. What was said to Miss Newfield?"

"Nothing, my Lord. I said that there were plenty of people out for the shoot, that the groundskeeper had some boys out helping around the place and that there might even be one or two from the village looking to poach." One shoulder lifted. "I believe that she accepted that as a reasonable excuse."

"That is good. Well done." Ringing the bell for the butler so that he might inform him about the gardener's increase in wages, David nodded his thanks. "If there is anything else that you see, or anything that you think is of importance, then I must ask you to inform me almost at once." He ran one hand over his forehead, screwing up his eyes for a second. "I had thought this danger long past. I did not think that it would return."

"Nor I, my Lord. I will, of course, do as you ask."

Taking his leave, the gardener stepped out just as the butler arrived. Quickly informing Burch of what was to happen as regarded the gardener, David then asked him to fetch Miss Newfield, telling him that she was to be shown in at once. The butler nodded and left the room, leaving David alone with his thoughts.

Why did this have to happen now, of all times?

Groaning, David put his head in his hands, his heart racing. If there was the same danger, if there was the same concern, then he would have to take swift action.

"It could be nothing." Speaking aloud, David made his way to the study window and looked out. "My mind is going directly to the very worst situation when I ought to be careful and considering."

Taking in three long, steadying breaths, he waited for his heart to slow itself and then lifted his chin as his eyes settled out the grounds outside. Part of him wanted to inform Miss Newfield that she was to keep Laura inside the house, whilst the other part of him said that he would be erring too much towards caution and that the restriction could frighten both Miss Newfield *and* his daughter.

"You do look rather troubled."

A soft voice caught his attention and David's heart leapt, suddenly and surprisingly, fully expecting to see Miss Newfield when he turned. Why he should think such a thing, he had very little idea, given that Miss Newfield would be, no doubt, in the schoolroom with Laura and, when his eyes met those of Lady Madeline, David was astonished at the sheer disappointment which crashed over him.

"What is wrong, my dear Lord Turton?"

Lady Madeline smiled at him, pushing the door closed and coming towards him.

"Lady Madeline, good morning." David cleared his throat and put his hands behind his back. "I do believe that I have spoken about this particular... situation already." He was not about to give in to a coy smile and dancing blue eyes. "You know that I would prefer that we refrain from any particular intimacy until we are wed."

"Ah, but that is not what *I* wish for," came the reply as she continued to move towards him. "And whilst I have thought about your request, I have decided that I must protest, in much the same way that I protested the shooting yesterday."

David's lips did not even flicker with a hint of a smile.

"I am aware that you were displeased but–"

"And why should I not be? The thought of being set apart from my betrothed for most of the day was most upsetting."

"But I am certain you had a most enjoyable day with the other ladies, did you not?"

The smile fell from her lips.

"It was not as enjoyable as being in your company, Lord Turton. I should hope that you feel the same."

David opened his mouth to respond, then closed it again quickly. He was not about to lie and state that he did harbor similar thoughts, nor was he about to be truthful and injure her feelings. Instead, he turned away and made his way to his desk, in what was a vain attempt to put some distance between them. For whatever reason, Lady Madeline seemed more than eager to be physically close to him and David was doing all he could to push that particular desire away for the present. "I will come to join my guests very soon. I have no intention of separating the gentlemen and ladies again today, which I am sure will be of great relief to you."

"It is." Lady Madeline smiled and came towards him, walking behind the desk so that she could stand behind him. Her hand rested on his shoulder, her fingers trailing along the back of his neck and David shivered despite himself. "We have not talked of the wedding as yet, however. When might we do so? Perhaps these few minutes would be a good opportunity?"

A good opportunity to tell her that I do not think I am eager still to wed?

"It is usual for most young ladies to have their marriage date already arranged! We are a little tardy, I fear."

David cleared his throat, twisting around in his seat so that he could look at her.

"It was a rather hasty arrangement, at the very end of the Season," he began, perhaps thinking that this could be used as a reason to reconsider their betrothal. "Perhaps –"

"Oh, I quite understand, and I do not hold such a delay against you. I was sure that we would arrange things while I was here. That was *certain* to be the reason that you invited both myself and my mother."

Taking a deep breath, David rose, turned, and grasped both of Lady Madeline's hands. He had to be honest. He had to tell her the truth – that he had been hasty and did not think that their marriage would make either of them at all happy.

"Lady Madeline, whilst I appreciate that our betrothal is now in place, I confess that I find myself struggling somewhat."

Her smile shattered, her blue eyes rounding.

"Struggling?"

"Our courtship was of a short duration. I proposed at the end of the Season, fearful that you would be caught by another should I delay for a year."

"Oh."

Much to his surprise, instead of looking at all upset, Lady Madeline immediately began to smile.

"I was caught by none but you, however."

"That may well be so, but I feel a lack of closeness between us. You do not know my character particularly well and I do not know yours."

She nodded.

"I concur, but such a thing can be easily resolved, for a husband and wife have a deep and intimate connection, do they not?" Smiling, she moved a little closer, her hands tightening on his, and instantly, David knew that he had not succeeded. Her head tilted back but David's heart still did not yearn for her, did not encourage him to drop his head and kiss her. Her rosebud lips parted gently, but all David heard was a warning, telling him to step back, to retreat else find himself tied to her forever.

"You sent for me, Lord –"

David spun on his heel, dropping Lady Madeline's hands, and seeing Miss Newfield's wide eyes staring back at him.

"Whatever is the meaning of this?" Lady Madeline threw up her hands and stalked around the desk towards Miss Newfield, who immediately shrank back in the face of her ire. "How dare you storm into Lord Turton's study?"

Much to David's horror, Lady Madeline raised a hand and slapped Miss Newfield directly across the face.

"*That* ought to teach you to be respectful of Lord Turton's authority!" Lady Madeline cried; her other hand curled into a fist. "Any maid of Lord Turton's should know her place! I am astonished that you would even *think* about walking into his study unannounced and I shall recommend highly that you are immediately dismissed!"

David's breath curled tightly in his chest, and he found himself frozen in place, staring at the scene unfurling before him. Miss Newfield's hand had gone to her cheek, her eyes wide with shock as she stared back at Lady Madeline.

"Why are you still here?" Lady Madeline flung out one arm towards the door, her finger pointing towards her. "Remove yourself from Lord Turton's presence until he requests you to enter."

Shock still wrapping itself around him, David began to hurry forward.

"Madeline, I –"

"First of all, I am no maid." Much to David's astonishment, Miss Newfield lifted her head, set her shoulders, and focused her sharp gaze on Lady Madeline. Her cheek was burning red but there was cold fury in her eyes. "I am the governess. Secondly, I was informed by the butler that I was expected in Lord Turton's presence, and I was to step into his study without delay." Her head lifted a little more.

"Therefore, I believe that I have obeyed Lord Turton and therefore I certainly do not deserve either to be struck nor to be dismissed."

Silence filled the room, sharp edges seeming to dig into David's skin. He knew that he ought to say something, but his mind was so overcome with shock that words seemed to entirely fail him.

Lady Madeline's reddening face turned towards him.

"Are you simply going to stand there, Turton?" Her voice was a furious whisper, her hands now pinned to her sides. "Are you going to allow your governess to speak to me in such a fashion?"

David grimaced, turning towards his betrothed.

"You should not have struck the lady, Madeline. She is quite correct. I asked the butler to send for her and to state that she should step into the room without hesitation." Seeing Madeline's eyes flare wide and the red in her cheeks now turn scarlet, he folded his arms across his chest. Whether he spoke in such a way in front of Miss Newfield or not, he could not allow Lady Madeline's actions to be considered appropriate. This was *not* the way that he treated his staff, and he certainly would not expect any wife of his to behave in such a fashion. "*You* were in the wrong." Coming closer, he gestured to Miss Newfield. "Miss Newfield did exactly as I asked and you, without consideration or thought, behaved callously and unfairly." Seeing his betrothed's eyes narrow, David continued, without hesitation, wondering if this incident might, in fact, be the catalyst that would end their betrothal. "You owe Miss Newfield an apology, Lady Madeline."

Lady Madeline's mouth dropped open.

"She is a governess!" she hissed, as though David was not already aware of her position. "You cannot expect–"

"Regardless of her position here, you have injured someone who did not deserve even the smallest rebuke," David insisted firmly. "In fact, Lady Madeline, when it comes to being in my company without permission or expectation, it is *you* who is in the wrong." The gasp which followed told David that he had shocked his future bride to the core. The color drained from her face and her hands fell limply to her sides. Without any regret filling his heart, David gestured to the door. Whether or not he would be forced into matrimony with Lady Madeline, she would have to know precisely the sort of gentleman he was – and he was one who would not stand quietly by when there was an injustice perpetrated, and nor would he permit any sort of cruelty. "We can continue our discussion another time, Lady Madeline. As you are now aware, I sent for Miss Newfield to discuss something of great importance." Lady Madeline blinked rapidly, tears forming in her eyes, but David's heart did not soften. "And if you will not apologize to Miss Newfield now, then I expect your apology to be given at a later time, as that is more than fair given what you did. I hope, Lady Madeline, that I have made myself quite clear."

It took a few moments but, eventually, Lady Madeline whirled out of the room in a flurry of skirts. The door closed hard behind her, and David was left standing with Miss Newfield.

His long sigh of both relief and frustration was more than a little audible.

"Her apology is not required, my Lord."

"It is." Speaking more sharply than he had intended, David threw Miss Newfield a quick glance. "You are a lady of quality, regardless of your current situation, and to have such an injustice thrust upon you is most unfair."

For whatever reason, David found himself reaching for her. His fingers touched her cheek, skimming lightly across the marks which Lady Madeline had put there.

"Oh!"

Miss Newfield flinched and turned her head away and David dropped his hand, suddenly embarrassed. Whatever had he been thinking? Making his way smartly back towards his desk, he stood behind it and then sat down, gesturing for Miss Newfield to come forward. She did so at once.

"As I have said, Miss Newfield. You did not deserve such treatment and I am sorry for it."

Her smile was sad, her eyes glistening gently as she came to stand in front of his desk.

"I may well be a lady of quality but, as you yourself have said, I must learn my new place. I am a governess now and such treatment, I fear, is to be expected."

"Not from me." Half out of his chair, David set both hands on the desk and leaned forward, wanting to reassure the lady. "I promise you, Miss Newfield, that you shall *never* have such treatment from me, nor will I ever permit it from another. There *will* be an apology, for it is the least that you deserve." Letting his gaze stray to the lady's cheek, he winced at the imprint of Lady Madeline's hand on Miss Newfield's skin. "That is not a behavior which I will tolerate."

"I hear that you are betrothed." Miss Newfield looked away, evidently attempting to change the subject. "That is wonderful. Does Laura know if it?"

A little uneasy, David sat back down.

"Miss Newfield, I would beg of you not to inform her."

The governess looked back at him directly.

"But of course. I will do as you wish."

A flare of surprise in her eyes caught his attention.

"My daughter does not know of the betrothal, and I am loath to inform her of it, given that it may not be of a long duration."

"Not of a long duration?" Immediately the governess dropped her head, looking away as her cheeks turned scarlet. Her head was lowered and her voice a little mumbled as she spoke. "Forgive me, my Lord. I should not have made such a remark."

David cleared his throat. Perhaps he ought not to have shared such a thing with the governess but yet, for whatever reason, he found himself wanting to tell her a little more.

"Pray, do not concern yourself unduly, Miss Newfield, for it was I who spoke a little more openly than I intended. For clarity, my betrothal was somewhat hasty, and therefore I have no intention of telling my daughter either of Lady Madeline's presence here or our betrothal."

Again, her eyes caught his.

"Are you considering ending the betrothal, my Lord?"

"It is something I am considering, yes." *Why do I find myself wanting to tell her everything?* Clearing his throat, he sat back in his chair, eyeing her. "Miss Newfield, is there a reason that you wished to talk to me this afternoon?"

A small, flickering smile caught the corner of her mouth and David found a gentle heat curling in his chest.

"I believe, my Lord, that it was you who sent for me."

"Ah." *I have become lost and distracted in what I wished to discuss with her.* The lingering red marks on Miss Newfield's cheek reminded him that it was Lady Madeline's presence that had caused such a disturbance. "Yes. I recall that it was to reassure you about the walk you took in the grounds yesterday afternoon with Laura."

Her eyes widened slightly, and her smile faded.

"My Lord?"

"The gardener informed me that you were a little perturbed during your time outdoors. I believe you were concerned that you saw somebody walking through the gardens."

"Yes, that is so, my Lord, but the gardener reassured me that it was someone from the hunt or perhaps a boy from the village who had come to poach."

"Precisely. He informed me of your concern, and I wanted to make certain that you were not afraid to step out of doors again."

Her lips curved into a gentle smile and David found himself smiling back. The softness in her eyes made his heart lift, realizing just how different she and Lady Madeline were, compared to each other. Lady Madeline could turn to harshness at any moment – astonishing even him, whereas Miss Newfield remained calm and astute, no matter the circumstances. What amazed him all the more was the gentle expression Miss Newfield wore, despite how harshly she had been treated by Lady Madeline only a few moments ago. There was something quite lovely about her character, despite the fact that he found her sometimes rather blunt and a little too forward for a governess.

"You are most considerate, my Lord."

"Thank you, Miss Newfield." Clearing his throat a little self-consciously, he looked away from her, unable to look into her eyes any longer due to the strange sensations which were beginning to swirl within his heart. "Obviously, I am most concerned about my daughter, and do not wish her to remain indoors for days on end."

Her smile faded

"But of course."

The awareness that his words had caused her smile to

shatter drove guilt into his heart, but David looked away, unwilling to be caught by such a strong emotion. It was not as though he could begin to consider the governess a friend, nor an acquaintance, even though she was a lady of quality. That would be most unsuitable. He had to remember that she was, first and foremost, his daughter's governess and, therefore someone in his employ. To view her as though she were a lady of the same social standing as himself would be a mistake.

And yet, David did not like that the blue in her eyes seemed to fade to grey. He took in her vivid red hair, pulled back from her face, but yet with a few wispy curls at her temples. For a brief moment, he let himself imagine what it would have been like to have met her in London, during the London Season. David acknowledged that she would have caught his attention. Her beauty was hidden somewhat by the governess' gown and the harsh bun which pulled her hair back so tightly, but David had to acknowledge that, even so, Miss Newfield had caught his attention –from their very first meeting!

"My Lord?"

Realizing that he had been staring at her – and that Miss Newfield was now gazing back at him curiously, David cleared his throat rather harshly.

"That is all, Miss Newfield."

Her gaze dropped to the floor, and she nodded.

"Thank you, my Lord."

"Oh, wait a moment." A little frustrated with himself, he beckoned her back to face him. "I recall, Miss Newfield, that you wished to speak to me about my daughter. I had promised you an opportunity to discuss matters with me and as yet, I believe, I have not done so."

A tiny, flickering smile caught her mouth and then was

gone at the very next moment. There was no happiness in it, but rather a sorrow that David knew was directed towards him.

"You have not, my Lord."

"I apologize. I have been rather caught up." Even to him his words sounded trite. Miss Newfield looked away and bit her lip as though she were fighting to keep her response entirely to herself. "I have been a little distracted but that is no reason to forget. My daughter is important to me, Miss Newfield."

"Is she?"

The steadiness in Miss Newfield's eyes astonished him. The question was impertinent, even for an acquaintance, but she showed no fear. Her brows lifted as she waited for his response, and David found himself struggling to come up with a reply.

"Of course, she is. Why should you think otherwise?"

His tone was hard, but that seemed to make no difference to the lady.

"Because I see no evidence of it, my Lord. I believe that I have mentioned such a thing before. I have been in your house some days and, as yet, I have never seen you in your daughter's company. I am aware that you have guests, but must you be with them every single moment?"

David licked his lips, caught somewhere between anger and shame. The way that Miss Newfield's eyes darted around the room told him precisely what she was thinking. Even with his guests present, he had spent plenty of time in his study. Why could he not have spent a few minutes with his daughter?

"You speak very plainly for a governess."

Miss Newfield shrugged.

"I will speak as I see. Your daughter misses you, I am

sure, even though she is unable, or unwilling, to express it. You say that you wish for her to speak, but you do not come to try to converse with her yourself. I can imagine it must be a little trying, given that there has been so much time apart, but that is all the more reason to try to rebuild the relationship between you, is it not?"

"And it does not help that I have given so little time to you and your request to discuss my daughter either, I suppose," David replied, begrudgingly, becoming quickly aware of his failings now that Miss Newfield had shone such a light upon them.

"You have given me no time at all, Lord Turton, save for the time that *you* have requested."

Wincing, David shook his head.

"That will do, Miss Newfield. You have made your point."

Miss Newfield dropped her head, her cheeks suddenly scarlet.

I do not mean to injure her.

It was on the tip of his tongue to apologize, but David closed his eyes for just a moment, tearing such thoughts into pieces.

"I shall remedy things at once. I have no time at the present to speak with you, but shall we say this evening?"

Her eyes flared in surprise.

"This evening?"

"I have entertainment for my guests, Miss Newfield," he explained, shrugging. "I can remove myself from it for a short while."

She nodded.

"But of course."

Her cheeks were still a little red, but her gaze returned to his.

"I will send for you." Gesturing to the door, he waited for her to take her leave, only for the lady to hesitate. Her lip caught between her teeth, and her fingers twined together as she glanced away for a moment, then let her gaze return to him. "Is there something else, Miss Newfield?" A small swirl of alarm began to rise in his chest. "Something of importance?"

Taking a deep breath, Miss Newfield let her shoulders relax.

"It is probably nothing of any significance given that you have reassured me about the figure I saw near the pond, but I–"

"Lady Madeline is waiting, and I am *certain*..."

The study door swung open, and Lord Carr swaggered through, his words and his steps coming to a sudden halt as he spotted Miss Newfield.

"I do beg your pardon, Turton."

Shrugging, he wandered towards the window, clearly having no intention of departing the room. After all, what could David say to a governess which could not be overheard by an acquaintance? Sighing inwardly, David gestured to the door.

"Thank you, Miss Newfield. I will speak with you again this evening." She exited the room without another word, leaving David alone with Lord Carr. Letting out a frustrated breath, David rose from his chair and gestured to the door. "Shall we make our way to the dining room?"

Lord Carr tilted his head, studying David.

"I am sorry if I interrupted your conversation. It is only that Lady Madeline has been waiting in the dining room for some minutes and is letting her frustration at your prolonged absence be known to everyone."

"I see."

Saying nothing more, David made his way to the door. His thoughts were not on Lady Madeline, but rather on Miss Newfield. What was it that she had been going to say? And why had there been a flicker of uncertainty in her eyes? Biting his lip, David made his way to the dining room. There was nothing else for him to do but wait until the evening - and yet that time seemed so very far away.

CHAPTER EIGHT

"Good night, my dear." Judith smiled at the little girl, smoothing one hand across her hair. "I do hope that you will have a restful sleep. You have done very well today."

The little girl smiled back at her before yawning widely, bringing one hand up to rub at her eyes. There had only been one whispered word today, but that had been more than enough for Judith. She had noticed that Laura had sat a little closer today and when they had been out walking, the girl's hand had reached for hers. Judith prayed that Laura was beginning to trust her and that soon, the conversation would begin to flow between them, even if it was only a few whispered words at a time.

"The man."

Judith looked at her charge, a frown forming.

"What do you mean, my dear?"

The little girl rubbed at her eyes again.

"The man at the pond."

This was more conversation than Judith had ever had

from the girl before, but she did not allow her excitement to overrule her concern.

"The man at the pond?" Again, she brushed Laura's hair from her cheek. "You are not frightened, are you? I spoke to the gardener and your father, and they both told me that he was meant to be there." Laura's eyes caught hers and Judith smiled as warmly as she could. "He was helping your father with the hunt."

The girl frowned.

"So close to the pond?"

Judith shrugged.

"I confess that I know very little about such things, but your father reassured me and now I can reassure you. You need not worry. Go to sleep, my dear girl, you are quite safe."

Laura did not close her eyes. Instead, the frown lingered, and she shook her head on the pillow.

"Mama was scared of the man."

Judith did not know what to say. Her breath curled tightly in her chest, but she tried to keep her smile fixed in place. On top of the fact that Laura was saying more to her than she had ever said before, there now came the realization that there was a deep and dreadful fear in Laura's heart over something that had happened in the past.

"I am sorry to hear that, but there is nothing for you to worry about. You are surrounded by people who love and care for you. The house is well protected. If you like, I can have your father come to talk to you about it?" Judith considered that Lord Turton would know more about this man and the worries which clung to Laura's mind. "Should you like him to do that?"

There came a short pause as Laura considered what Judith had asked. Then she shook her head, smiled, and reached up to brush her fingers across Judith's cheek. She did not say anything further, but her eyes began to close, and Judith smiled softly to herself despite her own inward concerns. At least Laura now felt safe enough to go to sleep. Whatever had been troubling her, she had been able to express it to Judith, and that, in itself, was almost a miracle.

Rising to her feet, Judith decided to take her leave of the child. It would not be long before Lord Turton requested her presence and Judith wanted to be prepared. Laura's breathing became slow and steady, telling Judith that she was already on the way to a night of deep sleep. Closing the door behind her, Judith took in a deep breath of her own, considering what it was that the girl had said.

Her mother?

Chewing her lip, Judith made her way back to the schoolroom. She had no idea who this man might be, nor why Lady Turton had been so afraid of him. Laura had only been a young child at the time, but that did not mean that she had not been aware of what had been going on. Or perhaps after her mother's death, she had overheard the staff talking. However, it had come about. Laura was clearly aware and afraid of a shadowy, unknown figure That was why the man at the pond had startled her so.

I shall have to inform Lord Turton.

Had she not been interrupted, Judith would have told Lord Turton about what she had witnessed the previous night. The way that he had responded to Lady Madeline's treatment of her had increased her trust in him all the more. He had not stood to one side and permitted Lady Madeline to treat her with disdain and callousness. Instead, he had come to her defense and had sent Lady Madeline away when *she* was his betrothed, and Judith was nothing more than a hired servant. Reaching up to run her fingers across her cheek. Judith let her mind go back to that moment. Lord Turton had proven himself to be a gentleman of honor. Despite the fact that Lady Madeline clearly expected him to stand with her, Lord Turton had sent her away without even a momentary hesitation. No doubt he had faced the lady's ire later that afternoon, but Judith was quite certain that he would have stayed steady in his determination that Lady Madeline had been in the wrong.

"And it appears he does not expect to marry the lady." Murmuring to herself, Judith wandered across the schoolroom, picking up the odds and ends which needed to be put back into place before the morrow. "How very strange."

It was most unusual for a gentleman to end his betrothal to a lady, and indeed, it could cause a great scandal if he was not careful. A wry smile pulled across her lips. After what she had witnessed of Lady Madeline today, she considered silently that Lord Turton and Lady Madeline were not suited in any way whatsoever. Yes, Lady Madeline was incredibly beautiful, but Judith did not see within her a beautiful character to match. From what she had observed and from what the servants had whispered, Lady Madeline appeared to be conceited, proud, and dreadfully selfish. On the other hand, Judith was beginning to consider Lord Turton a little more highly. Yes, he had been gruff, and yes, he had caused her upset on more than one occasion thus far, but he had also had the grace to apologize when he felt it necessary and had considered all that she had asked of him. At the same time, Judith knew that she was not as every other governess would be. She had much too sharp a tongue and was inclined to speak her mind without even a moment of hesitation. Such traits were not expected of a governess, and yet Lord Turton had permitted her to continue on in his house, regardless. Her smile grew as she recalled how

Lord Turton had made it plain. That had it not been for the house party, she might well have been returned home. Now she hoped that, once the house party came to an end, he would keep her in her position without any thought of sending her back to her brother. It was surprising to Judith that she felt such agony at even the thought of being separated from Laura. In such a short time, the girl had come to mean a great deal to her, and Judith could not imagine being sent away and never seeing her again. A sharp pain stabbed at her heart, and Judith stood up straight, catching her breath.

"Now I am being foolish." Her words echoed around the empty schoolroom. "There is nothing to fear." Her mind suddenly filled with thoughts of Lord Turton, recalling how he had looked at her today. Her skin had burned where his gentle fingers had brushed across her cheek, and she had felt such a strange warmth curling in her belly that she had been forced to turn away for fear that he would see in her eyes all that she now felt. It would be foolishness indeed to permit herself to feel anything for Lord Turton, given that he was not only a Marquess but, in fact, her employer. He had been the one to remind her, on more than one occasion, of her position in his household, and Judith was not about to do anything which would jeopardize that – not when the consequences of such actions would be more than a little detrimental.

"I must concentrate on my duties and my responsibilities to Laura."

Speaking with a little more firmness to herself, she collected the last remaining books and went to place them back on the shelf. This evening's discussion was meant to be only about Laura and her progress, as well as a little on her previous situation, but now Judith considered that there would be a good deal more to say. She would have to tell Lord Turton about Laura's whispered words as well as the fact that his daughter was afraid of the man who had been skulking near the pond. That, in turn, would lead to what Laura had said this evening and, whether or not Lord Turton chose to explain why Laura might say such a thing, Judith knew that she had a responsibility to inform him. She would also have to tell him about what she had seen the previous evening, even if it was nothing more than a guest arriving late or a servant scurrying back from some errand or other. She could only pray that Lord Turton would be able to spare the time to listen to everything that she had to say.

"If you will wait for a few moments, Miss Newfield, the master will be with you presently."

"But of course."

Judith sat down in one of the smaller chairs in the corner of Lord Turton's study and placed her hands in her lap. The study was lit by candlelight and Judith allowed her gaze to wander around the room. There was nothing of particular note, no personal items or trinkets. The study desk itself was clear, and Judith did not see a portrait of his late wife anywhere in the room. Perhaps it was that he had a miniature of her somewhere. Silently, Judith wondered what Lady Turton had been like. Had there been something about her character which had caused Lord Turton to send her away? Laura had said that her mother was afraid of a man and for a split second, Judith wondered if it had been Lord Turton himself. But the thought passed quickly, as Judith shook her head. That was a very dark thought indeed, and she would not permit herself to entertain it.

"I apologize, Miss Newfield."

Judith started as Lord Turton came into the room unexpectedly. Rising quickly from her chair, she bobbed a quick curtsey.

"Pray, do not apologize, my Lord, it was no trouble to wait."

"It is later than I had planned, and I should not like to take up your time unnecessarily." Much to Judith's surprise, Lord Turton did not go to sit behind his desk but rather took the chair next to her. His grey eyes were a little lighter, speaking of the excellent conversation and laughter he had been enjoying with his guests - and Judith could not help but feel a pang of envy. "Now, Miss Newfield, we are to speak of my daughter, are we not?"

Pushing away all thought of her previous life, where she had been allowed to enjoy soirees and the like, Judith nodded and centered her considerations on Laura.

"Yes, Lord Turton."

"Have you made any progress with her?"

Judith hesitated.

"In these first few days, I have tried only to become acquainted with her, Lord Turton. I have sought out her trust and I believe that I have begun to earn it." His brows lifted but Judith did not permit the surprise in his expression to hold her back. "I am well aware that you wish for your daughter to speak, and whilst that is important to me, also, I believe that I must first gain Laura's trust before she will be willing to talk with me openly." Leaning forward in her chair Judith spread her hands. "I will say, however, that she has spoken to me a little."

Lord Turton's eyebrows rose all the higher, and for some

moments it appeared that he could not speak. Blinking rapidly, he lowered his head for a few moments, took in a deep and audible breath, and then shook his head slightly.

"I do not think you know how much this means to me. Miss Newfield. My daughter has been practically silent since the moment that she arrived here, and now to hear that you have managed to have her speak within only a few days of your arrival is not only astonishing, but utterly, utterly wonderful." Lifting his head. He looked deeply into her eyes and Judith's breath caught in her chest at the intensity of his gaze. "I do not think I can ever find the words to express my gratitude, Miss Newfield."

"It has only been a few words. Lord Turton."

"That does not matter," he declared, suddenly reaching across and grasping her hand. "What you have achieved, Miss Newfield, is more than I had ever dreamed of - and in such a short time too." The tight grip of his fingers and the heat of his skin on her own was enough to send Judith's senses into turmoil. She forgot that she was talking about Laura, forgot all that they had been discussing. The look in his eyes was enough to keep her mesmerized; tied to him until he freed her from his spell. "Miss Newfield."

The huskiness in his voice sent fire shooting through her veins and no comprehensible thought came to her mind. Whatever was happening to her?

His thumb caressed the back of her hand, and Judith shivered. That movement seemed to snap Lord Turton out of his reveries, for he let go of her hand instantly, and sat back in his chair as he cleared his throat. The harsh guttural sound grated hard, and Judith dropped her gaze to the floor, suddenly embarrassed. It seemed safest to pretend that nothing had happened.

"Yes, my Lord?"

"You say that my daughter has spoken Miss Newfield. What is it that she has said to you?"

"Only one or two words, my Lord, but I believe that more will come in time."

Lord Turton nodded, his eyes searching hers.

"And do you think that she would speak to me"

Judith hesitated.

"I am not certain, my Lord. This has only just taken place and her words are very infrequent. However, I am sure that she would be willing to talk to you if you would only be patient."

A small, sad smile pulled at Lord Turton's lips.

"I am nothing if not patient, Miss Newfield."

Pressing her lips together, Judith considered what it was she wanted to say.

"Lord Turton, I tell you this only so that you are aware, rather than seeking any explanation. This evening Laura informed me that she was afraid of the man at the pond and when I sought to reassure her, she then went on to say that her mother had been afraid of a man."

Aware that she ought to be looking away, Judith was unable to prevent her gaze from lingering on Lord Turton, wishing to see his reaction. For a moment the gentleman stared at her as though he could not quite believe what had been said. A long breath escaped him, and he dropped his head, his fingers burrowing through his hair as his elbows rested on his knees. Judith sucked in a breath, aware now, from his reaction, that there was something significant about the man she had seen.

I do not require any explanation, she reminded herself. *It is not my place to know.*

Lord Turton let out a hissing breath, but remained precisely as he was.

"I did not think that my daughter had ever been aware of..." His words trailed to nothing, and he kept his head low, leaving Judith to wonder what it was he had not said. It was not only her curiosity that was piqued, but also her concern - not only for Laura, but for Lord Turton. "Are you quite sure that was what she said?"

His head lifted suddenly, and Judith nodded, caught by the fervency in his eyes.

"Yes, my Lord, I am quite certain."

"Might I ask what it is that you said in response to this?"

Suddenly afraid that she had done wrong, Judith spread her hands.

"I knew nothing of the situation, my Lord, so I only reassured her that she was safe within your house." He nodded, looking away. "I believe that seeing the man by the pond has frightened your daughter. I do not know the cause, but I thought it best to inform you, particularly given that I also saw someone scurrying across the garden only yesterday evening – I intended to mention that to you earlier before our conversation was interrupted. I am sure it was only a tardy guest or someone belonging to the household, but I am afraid that if Laura sees something such as that, then her fear may only grow."

Judith was not prepared for Lord Turton's reaction. His eyes flared wide, and his hands reached out and took hold of hers, pulling her upwards. Staggering, Judith fell hard against him, but Lord Turton quickly caught her arms, pushing her back a little and holding her steady. His grey eyes searched her face, his jaw tight and lines furrowing across his brow.

"What did you see?"

His voice was low and commanding. An unspoken fear began to etch itself across his face, and Judith could not help but respond to it. A shudder run across her frame, but Lord Turton's fingers only clasped tighter onto her arms.

"It is just as I have said, my Lord. I saw someone walking across the gardens in what I thought to be a furtive manner. It was late last evening, just before the sunset." Swallowing hard, she looked up into his face. "I told myself that I was being quite ridiculous, and that I was only thinking such things due to the scare I'd had, earlier in the gardens with Laura. I... I am sorry if I did the wrong thing, Lord Turton, in not informing you of this sooner. As I have said, I believed it was only my own fears, rather than anything of particular importance."

Lord Turton did not respond immediately. Instead, his eyes continued to search her face as though she was holding something back from him, which he could not yet determine. Licking her lips, Judith looked back into his eyes, silently demanding that her heart begin to quieten itself from its current furious thundering.

"There was no tardy guest last evening. Miss Newfield." Lord Turton let out a long breath, but his hands did not release themselves from her arms. "None of the staff should have been out in the garden so late in the evening. Some of them may have had a few hours reprieve after the dinner, but they would have exited through the servant's entrance rather than walking through the gardens." Judith nodded, but remained silent. Lord Turton's furious reaction had astonished her. "Might you be able to describe this person, Miss Newfield? Was there anything about him which appeared particularly conspicuous?"

Wishing that she could give him a better answer. Judith dropped her head.

"No, my Lord. I was at the schoolroom window and, as such, could not make out his face."

"Then might I ask what made you believe that he was acting in a furtive manner?"

Hesitating for a moment, Judith considered her answer.

"This person, whoever he was, did not appear to be making his way directly to the front door. It was as though he did not wish to be seen, for he moved from one place to the next with quick, hasty movements and his steps as I have said, were not direct." One shoulder lifted it in half-shrug, held back somewhat by Lord Turton's grip. "It did seem rather strange to me, but I told myself that it was only my lingering concern from the afternoon's walk in the gardens with Laura." Seeing Lord Turton's frown grow all the more. Judith dropped her gaze again. I am sorry if I made the wrong choice in not coming to you at the time, my Lord. Given that I have already interrupted you on more than one occasion - and particularly during your house party - I thought it best to remain silent. I believed, whether wrongly or rightly, that you would consider my concerns foolish."

Lord Turton's hands gently released from her shoulders, but they did not fall to his sides. Instead, they slid slowly down her arms until his fingers finally caught hers. The fire which had burned through her veins only moments ago returned with such a fierceness that Judith could not help but catch her breath. The gasp, she was sure, was overheard by Lord Turton, for his eyes suddenly flared and the frown on his forehead began to lift. Silence fell, but the air was thick, and Judith struggled to breathe at a steady pace. Butterflies began to fill her stomach as Lord Turton twined his fingers with hers, holding her fixed in place. Quite what he was thinking, Judith could not see, for her mind was filled with so many questions that she could not begin to separate one from the other. Along with such thoughts came a warning, a warning that she could not help but pay attention to. It would not be the first time that a governess had been taken advantage of by the master of the house. Such things were not spoken of but were well known within the *ton* and, given that she was now a governess, Judith knew she had to be on her guard.

And yet, I do not wish to pull away.

"How is your cheek?"

It was a strange question, and it shattered the confusing silence which had surrounded them for the last few moments. Judith turned her head, looking away from him. Was this why he was holding her hands? Had he realized just how unsuitable Lady Madeline was for him, and was now using this closeness to imagine what it would be like to be with another?

"You need not concern yourself, Lord Turton. I am quite well."

"I fear there will be a bruise."

His voice was soft, and Judith let the concern in his voice bind itself around her heart.

"There shall not be a bruise," she replied, speaking with more certainty than she felt. "Please Lord Turton, do not worry, there is enough for you to consider at the present moment, I am sure."

This seemed to remind Lord Turton of what they had been speaking about, for he nodded, stepped back, and finally released her hands.

"I will not go into particular details. Miss Newfield, but needless to say, if you ever see such a thing again, I wish for you to inform me of it at once."

"Yes, I shall." Hesitating she took a small step nearer to him and saw his eyes alight to hers. "I will not ask for an explanation. Lord Turton. It is only to ask if Laura is safe walking on the grounds? I should always be with her, of course."

When he did not answer immediately. Judith's fears began to grow. They spread like a darkness through her, sending her breath spiraling in her chest as a heavy weight settled in her stomach, pulling her towards the ground.

"I think Miss Newfield, it would be for the best if you took someone with you when you next stepped outside with Laura. They do not need to be directly next to you, but should watch both yourself and my daughter at all times. I will ask the gardener to make certain that he is present, but perhaps a footman also." Now a small smile tugged at the corner of his mouth and the tension which held Judith so tightly began to loosen. "I myself will accompany you tomorrow. I may have guests, but my daughter is of much greater importance. I should have seen such a thing before, but I see it very clearly now."

Judith swallowed hard. There was an unseen menace that she had been, and was still mostly unaware of, and yet there came as a result, a relief that Lord Turton would be present, ready to protect them both from whatever this threat was. It was not her place to demand an explanation, but she prayed that in time, Lord Turton would be willing to tell her all.

CHAPTER NINE

"Do come in." Sighing inwardly, David waited as his butler stepped into the room. "Yes, Burch?" Lifting one eyebrow, he waited for his butler to respond, and was a little surprised when the man clasped both hands in front of him and looked away. This was most unlike the fellow. "Burch." David spoke a little more firmly. "I am soon to go to my guests - whatever the matter is, pray tell me at once."

Finally, the Butler met his gaze.

"My Lord, Lady Madeline is requesting a visit to the mistress' rooms." For a moment, David did not understand. His lack of clarity must have shown in his expression for the butler continued to explain. "The rooms once occupied by Lady Turton." Clearing his throat, he looked away once more. "Lady Madeline insists that you have given her permission to walk through each of the rooms. She stated that I did not need to disturb you and assured me that it was simply so that when the time came, she knew what she wished to do with the current décor and the like." The man's shoulders rounded. "I confess, my Lord, that I was quite unaware of any agreement that you had made with the lady and thus thought it best to come and confirm such arrangements with you." The man spread his hands, shifting from one foot to the other. "I can only apologize if I have misstepped. That was not my intention."

David was unprepared for the swell of anger which rose within him. It gripped him tightly, causing pain to ripple up through his chest. Gritting his teeth, he closed his eyes and took a deep breath. The last thing he needed to do was to lose his temper in front of his staff. They did not need to know that Lady Madeline had upset him so greatly.

Whatever does she think she is doing?

There had not been even the smallest conversation on this matter, and Lady Madeline had lied outright. Perhaps she had believed that the butler would not come to confirm such things with him, given the fact that she was soon to be mistress of this house. Regardless, David was even more angry with himself that he had ever thought a betrothal between them was the right step. Looking back, he saw now just how captured he had been by her beauty, despite the fact that he had known nothing of her character. Had he given himself only a few more days, David was sure that he would have quickly realized that Lady Madeline was not a wise choice for a bride.

"Thank you for informing me, Burch."

The butler's head lifted.

"What am I to do, my Lord?"

"You are not to allow Lady Madeline into any of my late wife's rooms."

Those rooms had been unoccupied for some years, but David was still unwilling to allow Lady Madeline entry. Indeed, Lady Turton had only been present in those rooms for a short while after their marriage, but David was not about to let Lady Madeline consider any of them her own. It seemed that, despite the difficulties of the previous day, Lady Madeline was still very eager to wed him, given her behavior.

"Very well, my Lord."

The slight tremor in the butler's voice told David a good deal more than the man verbally expressed.

"Wait a moment." David drummed his fingers lightly on the table. "This is not your responsibility, Burch. If Lady Madeline insists otherwise, then you must come to inform me at once, and I shall deal with her directly."

A flash of relief crossed the butler's eyes and his shoulders dropped.

"Thank you, my Lord."

"Of course."

Waiting until the butler had closed the door tightly behind him. David dropped his head forward into his hands and let out a long exhale of breath. As yet, he had not been able to speak to Lady Madeline about what she had done to Miss Newfield, and David could practically see the mountain growing between them. He would have to speak to her directly. Had he not already decided that this betrothal had been a mistake? Had he not already thought of ways to end their attachment? Why, then, was he finding reasons to remain both far from Lady Madeline and silent?

Pressing the palms of his hands against his eyes, David drew in a long breath. When he had been with Miss Newfield the previous evening, there had been such a spark between them that he had felt as though embers from the fire had singed his clothes and burned his skin. The depths in her beautiful blue eyes had called to him and he had longed to reach forward and take her into his arms. Quite what he had wished to do thereafter, David was still uncertain, but there had been an openness and gentle understanding in her which David found a soothing balm to his troubled heart. Of course, he had not told her the truth, but Miss Newfield had not demanded it from him. Lady Madeline demanded much. They were the exact opposite of each other and in his heart, David knew which of them he was drawn to.

I cannot allow myself to be pulled toward a governess. Despite the fact that Miss Newfield was the daughter of a Viscount, David was all too aware of her position in his household. After all, he was the one who had pointed out that she ought to behave in the manner required of a governess!

But that does not mean that I cannot be honest with Lady Madeline.

Thumping one hand down on the table, he pushed his chair back and rose from his desk just as the door opened and Lady Madeline herself stepped inside, with the butler following hastily thereafter. Her face was scarlet and her eyes blazing with an inner, furious fire whilst Burch's own face was also red as stammering words poured from his mouth.

"Be silent!" With a swipe of her hand, Lady Madeline cut through the air, demanding silence from the Butler. "Turton, your staff are lying to me, and I am most displeased!"

"You may go, Burch."

The butler's eyes flared, but he did not question the matter, stepping out of the study at once.

"Madeline, be silent." David let his voice boom across the room and watched as Lady Madeline's eyes flared with astonishment. Much to his relief, she did remain silent thereafter although her color stayed high.

"I assume that you are coming to tell me that the Butler has refused you entry into my late wife's rooms." Lifting one eyebrow. David saw the awareness in his betrothed's eyes and the hard line setting her mouth. "In this case, Lady Madeline, the butler has not told you any mistruths. It is precisely as I have ordered."

Lady Madeline's mouth opened as though she meant to speak, but David held up one hand, silencing her. "In fact, I believe it is *you* who has been telling mistruths. You have told my staff that you have my consent to parade through those rooms as and when you wish. But the truth of the matter is that I have never allowed you such a thing."

Her hands at her hips, Lady Madeline's eyes narrowed as she glared back at him.

"That is not at all the case. When we were in London, you promised me that I could –"

"I will not be manipulated!" Coming around from behind his desk, David stood only a few feet away from the lady. "There are many things which I said in London, Lady Madeline, but I can assure you that I never once promised that you should be able to walk through my late wife's rooms with a view to changing them to your own preferences."

"But why should I not?" It appeared now that Lady Madeline realized her anger was doing nothing to garner David's sympathy. Her voice was wheedling, her hands clasped in front of her, no longer pressed hard against her hips. "I am to be your wife, and I am to be mistress of this house. Why should you deny me such a thing?"

Struggling to hold back his temper, David threw up his hands.

"You did not even think to ask me, Lady Madeline. You decided to do this of your own accord! You act without consideration to others. You believe that you are always in the right and, for whatever reason, you seem to expect me to always oblige you."

Lady Madeline's chin lifted, and David could see the pride in her eyes.

"Why should you not oblige me? You are meant to be my husband and a husband dotes upon his wife."

A small creeping smile began to pull at one side of her lips and David found himself repulsed.

"That is only if there is something to dote upon, my dear lady." Unable to keep the harshness from his voice, David saw the smile begin to slip from Lady Madeline's face. "When we were in London, I thought that I was in love with you. I see now that it was nothing more than a brief affection based solely upon the beauty before me. I trusted that your heart was just as beautiful, and unfortunately, I now begin to realize just how wrong I was in that assumption."

"How dare you?" Lady Madeline's face went sheet white, her hands clenched, and a tightness came into her frame which lifted her shoulders. A spot of deep red appeared in each cheek as she stalked towards him, one finger pressed hard into his chest. "We are betrothed. You will not speak to me in that way."

"We are not betrothed."

This was not how David had wanted to end their betrothal, but right here, in this one single moment, he knew that he could not tie himself to her for a second longer.

Lady Madeline's hand dropped. Her eyes rounded and she stared back at him.

"Whatever can you mean?"

There was no anger in her voice now.

"It is precisely as I have said." Lifting his chin, David held her gaze steadily. "I believed that our marriage would be a happy one. I believed that you were the most kind, most beautiful creature in all of England. I was completely mistaken, and for that I am sorry. I cannot marry you, Lady Madeline. It would bring us both a great deal of unhappiness and that is not a future I am not willing to risk – not just for myself, but also for my daughter."

"Your daughter?" Lady Madeline's lip curled. "You have said very little about your daughter to me. She has never been a consideration before this moment."

Her breathing was quick and fast, her harshness designed to do nothing more than injure him.

"That is not true."

Lady Madeline's words pricked at his conscience and David recoiled inwardly. As much as he did not want to admit it, there was a truth in what she said, echoing Miss Newfield's words also. Laura had not been a consideration when it had come to David's betrothal. He had pulled himself away from that situation, away from his daughter, because the pain had been too great. Even though she was now a part of his household, he had not made any attempt to go to her. All he had thought about was his own happiness and circumstances. He realized, in one hot, horrifying moment, that he had been so very wrong. His daughter needed him, and he had failed her. Telling himself that he was protecting her, he had stepped to one side and left her to the care of his staff.

"I can tell that you see truth in my words. You are using your daughter as an excuse."

Triumph shone in her eyes and David shook his head, steeling himself inwardly.

Whether she is right or wrong, now is not the time for such considerations. Drawing in a deep breath, David turned his full attention back at Lady Madeline.

"That may have been true in the past, Lady Madeline, but will not be so now. In looking to the future, I *must* consider not only my daughter but also my own happiness. We would not be happy together. You are much too selfish, much too prideful. I fear that I would lose every single one of my servants, should you become mistress of this house. Should we marry, I fear that I would regret it every single day for the rest of my life. Therefore, Lady Madeline, we shall not wed. I am breaking our betrothal."

Lady Madeline's rosebud lips were gently parted, her breathing shallow with her eyes wide in horror. It was as though she could not believe that David had chosen to step away from her.

"You cannot." Her voice was hoarse, her words ragged. "You cannot end our betrothal. We are due to wed. My father is expecting the details to be sent to him very soon. All of London knows of our betrothal. The *ton* has not stopped speaking of it since it became known! They have called you the luckiest of all the gentlemen in England, given that you and you only have secured my hand – I, who am considered a diamond of the first water. You cannot throw me aside now!"

David folded his arms across his chest, unmoved by her plight.

"All that you have said may be true, Lady Madeline, but my mind will not be changed. I will not marry you."

A great sense of freedom filled his chest and he breathed deeply, wanting to spread his arms wide, throw his head back and squeeze his eyes closed with relief. Instead, he remained precisely where he was. This conversation would soon have to be brought to an end, for he would not be drawn into an argument with her. His decision had been made.

"And what reason will you give?" Lady Madeline's eyes were glassy. "What shall you say was the reason for ending our betrothal?"

"Simply the truth." David spread his hands. "That during the house party we both realized that we would not be well suited. We shall tell our friends and acquaintances that it was a decision we made together so that neither of us bears the blame. There will be no scandal and the news of our betrothal ending will be but a breath – gone in a moment." Seeing the sudden spark in her eyes, a warning rang in David's mind. His brows lowered, his eyes a little hooded. "But know this, Lady Madeline. Should you speak lies about me, then nothing will prevent me from telling *my* truth to my friends and acquaintances. Otherwise, I shall remain quite civil, with the expectation that you shall be so also."

Lady Madeline sniffed, drawing herself up. She looked him square in the eye, but her chin wobbled slightly.

"You have broken my heart, Lord Turton, and now you pain me all the more by suggesting that I might speak mistruths about you!"

Her defense of her character was not unexpected, and David chose to remain silent rather than refute her remarks. His eyes beheld her as she truly was - a lady without substance, who thought only of her beauty and her standing, who expected those around her to meet her every whim and fancy. Such words meant nothing to him. He did not believe that her heart was broken, nor that her tears were for the affection she had lost. Rather, it came solely from her injured pride. How glad he was that he had found the courage to end their betrothal. There was to be no future for them any longer and, as he considered that glorious truth, nothing but relief swamped him.

"You are, of course, welcome to remain at the house party until it ends." Gesturing to the door, he lifted one eyebrow. "Although I quite understand if you wish to depart. However, Lady Madeline, I should remind you that you also still need to apologize to Miss Newfield."

"Miss Newfield!"

Lady Madeline spat her name back at him.

"You care too much for that governess! You come to her defense instead of to mine and think more highly of her than you do of your betrothed."

"We are no longer betrothed, Lady Madeline." Giving her a small bow, he stepped back, ready to return to his desk and continue with his correspondence. "Good afternoon."

It took some moments for Lady Madeline to leave the room. She stared at him for a long time, her hands at her hips, her eyes narrowed as she waited for him to respond to her stare. It was as if she expected him to say something more, as though she thought that he would suddenly turn around and change his mind. Did she truly believe that he would fall to his knees and beg her to return, to forget entirely the last few moments and the decisions which he had made? Determined to remain silent, David picked up his quill, bent over his letters, and began to write, making it quite clear that the conversation was at an end. It was only then, listening hard, that he heard her soft footsteps make their way to the door, and heard the door itself open, creaking gently on its hinges. When it closed behind her, David dropped his quill to the paper, threw his head back, and let out a long breath of relief.

He was free.

CHAPTER TEN

"I did tell your father that you have begun to speak to me." Judith looked steadily back into Laura's eyes, seeing the solemness in the little girl's expression. "You need not fear, however. He will not demand that you speak to him also."

Laura nodded slowly, worrying her lip as Judith smiled back at her.

"It is very good of him to step out and walk with us today," she continued, injecting as much happiness into her voice as she could. "Where should you like to go?" Waiting for Laura to respond, Judith was not surprised when the little girl dropped her head. There was probably a reluctance to say anything given her surprise that Lord Turton was to join them, as well as a lingering fear over what – or who – might be out in the gardens with them. "Should you like to go to the rose garden again?"

After a moment, Laura shook her head.

"Then mayhap we should walk to the other end of the gardens. I have been told that there is a little fountain pond there, where one might find some peace and quiet. Tell me, are there fish there also?"

A small smile crept across Laura's face, and she nodded. A spark of interest caught her eyes and she grasped Judith's outstretched hand.

"Very good. Then let me inform Lord Turton where we are to go, and he will join us when he is ready." Taking Laura by the hand, she stepped out into the hallway, walked to the stairs, and quickly found a footman. The man disappeared, ready to relay her message to Lord Turton, and Judith continued to make her way downstairs. They were both wearing their warm shawls for, whilst it was a beautiful autumnal day, Judith suspected that it would be cold. Keeping her chin lifted and her smile fixed to her lips for Laura's sake, Judith could not help but feel a swell of uncertainty. A nervous anxiety ran through her veins, and her stomach twisted this way and that, as thoughts of her previous conversation with Lord Turton ran through her mind. Questions began to fill her head and she glanced down at Laura. She did not want Laura to feel at all discomposed stepping outside, but Judith was all too aware that there was a real and genuine threat of which, as yet, she had no knowledge.

"Let us wait a moment." Seeing Laura's large eyes look up at her, Judith smiled. "Your father may be ready to join us at once and it would do us no good to step out without him. The footman will return soon to inform us."

The very moment she finished speaking, Lord Turton's voice echoed down the hallway towards her.

"Ah, there you are. I have just received your message from the footman. I am quite ready and able to join you."

The stirrings in Judith's stomach only increased as Lord Turton drew towards them, and she dropped her gaze, focusing on her charge instead. Laura's hand tightened perceptibly on her own and, as Lord Turton came closer, she turned to hide her face in Judith's skirts.

Judith licked her lips, uncertain what she was to do next. Her instincts told her that to push Laura into conversation with her father would be of no benefit to the child, but she feared that this was Lord Turton's expectation.

"Good afternoon, Laura." Lord Turton spoke directly to his daughter, looking down at her. "We are to take a walk together. I do hope that pleases you."

Laura did not move but her fingers curled tighter into Judith's hand. Lord Turton sent a confused look towards Judith, but she merely shook her head. Without giving any further explanation, she waited for Lord Turton's reaction. Would he demand that his daughter look at him? That she speak? After a few moments – and much to her surprise - the man merely closed his eyes, sighed, and nodded.

"I have not been a devoted father." His honest words tore at Judith's heart. "It does not surprise me, my dear child, that you have no willingness to even look at me. I do not hold it against you." A sad smile spread across his face as he lifted his head and looked directly at Judith. "I have a great deal to consider when it comes to my daughter, Miss Newfield. I have not been thoughtful or considerate. I see it now. Your words have been blunt and hard to accept, but they have also been the truth. The way that I have been, I hope, will no longer be the case. Perhaps these walks can become a daily occurrence?"

The ache which came into Judith's heart was not one of pain, but rather one of gladness and relief.

"I am sure that both myself and Laura would appreciate your company, my Lord." A sudden embarrassment washed over her as she realized what she had expressed. It was true that she would be glad of Lord Turton's company but that, she told herself, was only because of the safety that his presence would bring. "That is to say, my Lord, I would be glad to have you walk with us simply because of..." She trailed off, realizing that she could not say anything further due to Laura's presence. "I am sure we would both be glad of your presence."

Lord Turton chuckled, and Judith's embarrassment grew, to the point that she looked away, unable to even glance at him.

"Come, then. Let us take the air."

Gesturing to the door Lord Turton stepped to one side as Judith led Laura out. There was a bite to the air, but Judith was glad that the chill calmed her red cheeks.

"I think that Laura would like to go to visit the fountain." Setting her hand on Laura's shoulder, Judith smiled as Laura glanced up at her. "Is that not so?"

It took a moment, but eventually the girl nodded. Her eyes drifted towards Lord Turton, but he only smiled, then spoke softly, hopefully, his eyes on Laura.

"Then, we are to go to the fountain?"

Judith pressed Laura's shoulder gently, silently encouraging her. A gentle pink burned across Laura's cheeks but there was no fear in her eyes.

"Yes."

The single whispered response brought such a look of delight to Lord Turton's face that Judith could not help but laugh with the sheer joy of it. Lords Turton's eyes rounded but his face split into such a wide grin that his happiness was unmistakable. What made the moment all the more beautiful was that Laura herself let out a little giggle, turned, and then began to run across the grass directly towards the fountain. Judith made to call out after her, wanting her to walk alongside herself and Lord Turton, but the gentleman quickly grasped her arm.

"Pray do not." His fingers brushed across her wrist as he pulled back his hand. "She is happy. I am happy. Happier than I think I have been in some time." Shaking his head, he let out a long, low whistle. "I can hardly believe that she spoke to me. I think you quite remarkable, Miss Newfield."

"I have done very little," Judith protested, falling into step beside him as they followed after Laura. "It may be that she would have spoken to you regardless. Perhaps all that was required was a little more time."

"No, I am certain that your gentle and sweet spirit has had a great deal to do with my daughter's recovery." Shaking his head, his smile began to fade. "It is also my own fault for not realizing just how much she understood the situation. As I have said, Miss Newfield, I have not been the most present of fathers."

"A situation you intend to remedy, however," she reminded him, not wishing him to be lost in regret. "Within a week or so, I fully expect Laura to be speaking to you regularly, my Lord."

The urge to ask him what it was he meant about the previous situation burned on her tongue, but Judith did not allow those questions to drop from her lips.

"I have ended my betrothal." Shock jarred through Judith's frame, and she could not prevent her gasp. "You are surprised. You are not the only one who will be surprised when I have informed them of my actions." A wry smile crossed his lips as his eyes met hers. "You are the first person I have told, Miss Newfield."

Why is the master of the house informing me of such a thing? Why should he want me to know?

A sudden flurry of hope filled her heart, but Judith

ignored it. She could not allow herself to begin to believe foolishness.

"I do hope that you will find contentment in your decision, Lord Turton."

"I believe I already have, Miss Newfield, although I appreciate the sentiment. My conversation with Lady Madeline last evening was not a particularly easy one, but in the course of that conversation I soon realized that I was not the father I had hoped to be. I had allowed myself to become distracted by Lady Madeline's beauty, thought only of my own circumstances, and allowed my own hopes to take hold of my heart. The circumstances surrounding my late wife's death were painful and, whilst I believe that I truly thought I was doing the very best for my daughter, I see now that I did not give any real thought to what she was feeling."

Keeping a close eye on Laura as she ran ahead towards the fountain, Judith started as her fingers brushed Lord Turton's.

"I do beg your pardon." They were walking so very close that it was almost impossible for such a thing not to have happened and a single glance towards Lord Turton told Judith that he was not at all perturbed. In fact, he was smiling. "There is a – oh!" All embarrassment and awkwardness suddenly fled as Judith's eyes fastened onto the sight of a figure walking across the gardens. He appeared to be making his way towards Laura, and the child had not yet seen him coming. Fear began to tie itself in knots in Judith stomach, and her fingers grasped hold of Lord Turton's arm. "My Lord!" Her other hand stretched out, her finger pointing. "Is that the gardener?"

They had come to a standstill as Judith's eyes narrowed, trying to make out the figure. Blood roared in her ears and her fingers gripped all the tighter to Lord Turton's arm.

"Laura!"

Lord Turton's loud voice boomed out across the garden and the child turned immediately. Judith dropped her hand as Lord Turton began to stride towards the girl, hurrying to keep up with him.

"Come and walk with us."

No hint of fear entered Lord Turton's voice, but Judith could tell by his quick steps and hasty movements that he was concerned. Much to her relief, Laura did precisely as was requested, running back towards them. Instead of going to Lord Turton, however, she grasped Judith's hand and leaned in towards her. Judith let out a slow, quiet breath of relief, but Lord Turton's attention was still on the figure who had been walking towards Laura.

"Wait here, Miss Newfield."

Lord Turton began to stride towards the figure, calling aloud for him to wait a moment. Turning Laura away from the sight, Judith began to wander in the opposite direction, worried that what the child might see would frighten her all the more. As yet, Laura appeared to be entirely unaware that there was anything of concern occurring. Glancing over her shoulder, Judith watched as Lord Turton approached the man. Lord Turton's hand reached out – but then, to her utter shock, the man turned on his heel and began to run. A shout tore from Lord Turton's lips as he gave chase, but the man had already gained the advantage. With long strides, he ate up the ground until finally he disappeared into the trees on the left-hand side of the gardens. Those trees led to a forest and the forest led to the village, where the man might mingle with the locals and soon disappear entirely. Lord Turton seemed aware of such a thing also, for he came to a stop at the edge of the trees and put his hands on his thighs, bending forward slightly. Continuing to wander aimlessly, with Laura by her side, Judith glanced over her shoulder again, seeing Lord Turton standing there silently for some moments as he caught his breath.

Then he turned back towards them.

"The fountain?" Putting a brightness into her voice that she did not feel, Judith looked down as Laura glanced up. "Your father is about to return to join our company." The child was smiling, her eyes bright and her cheeks red and rosy. She was entirely unaware of what had just taken place and that, at least, was a relief. "And here comes your father back to join us. I am sure that he is finished speaking with the gardener by now."

Judith widened her eyes as Lord Turton's dark expression caught her attention. A swift glance towards Laura and then back towards him seemed to make him understand what she was trying to silently say, for his smile returned, albeit rather dimly.

"We are to go to the fountain together?" Judith inquired.

After a moment Lord Turton nodded and held out his hand towards his daughter. Silently willing Laura to accept, Judith smiled her encouragement as the girl glanced up at her and ignored the fury with which her heart was currently beating. After a moment, Laura raised one tentative hand and gently placed it in her father's, whilst the other clung to Judith's.

"Yes, we shall walk to the fountain together." Lord Turton's voice was low and one look at him told Judith that this matter had suddenly become very serious indeed. "Forgive me for my absence, I had an urgent matter to discuss with the groundsman."

"With the gardener," Judith corrected, her eyes flaring as Lord Turton shot her a confused glance. When she widened her eyes, he merely nodded. "I do not think we will be able to stay out for long, however. The afternoon is colder than I had thought it." Squeezing Laura's hand, she saw the girl's bright smile and felt her heart sink. What difficulty was the child in? "Are you feeling a little cold, Laura? I confess that my shawl is not as warm as I had hoped!"

"I am not."

Laura's words were no longer a whisper but rather spoken aloud with a great deal more confidence than Judith had ever expected to hear. A giggle broke from her lips and Judith could not help but laugh despite her inward anxiety. Lord Turton looked down at his daughter, his smile lifting the corner of his lips. There was a happiness in his eyes that could not be mistaken, despite the strange and unsettling circumstances and that, in itself, brought her a measure of relief. It was as though, in ending his betrothal to Lady Madeline, Lord Turton had finally realized the sort of gentleman he wished to be. In his discussion with Lady Madeline, he had seen his mistakes and become aware of his failures in his relationship with his daughter, and was now quite determined to change – and despite this only being their first time out walking together, Judith found herself believing him completely.

"Perhaps, Miss Newfield, you and I might talk as my daughter searches for fish in the fountain?"

Judith nodded, catching the resignation in his eyes. It was clear that he did not wish to talk to her about these matters, but given what they had just witnessed, it seemed that he now had no choice. As they approached the fountain, Lord Turton bent down and smiled into his daughter's face.

"Did you know that there are many little fish in this fountain? When I was a boy, my father used to challenge my brother and I to count them all, although now that I think of it, we never really agreed on the number!"

Judith's heart lifted as Laura's giggle reached her ears.

"Do you think that you might do a better job than I? Might you be able to count all the fish in the fountain?"

Laura stuck one finger in her mouth but nodded. Looking inquiringly up at Judith with her light green eyes, she waited until Judith nodded, smiling her encouragement.

"On you go then." Releasing Laura's hand, Judith pushed her gently towards the fountain. "I will remain here with your father for a short while."

Her eyes followed the girl as she ran towards the fountain, her smile a little sorrowful. Laura was entirely unaware of the danger which presented itself, and whilst Judith was grateful for that, she was all the more concerned for Laura's safety.

Lord Turton cleared his throat and the sound interrupted Judith's considerations.

"It seems, Miss Newfield, that I am to tell you all, regardless of my intention to stay quiet on the matter."

"I am more than willing to listen, my Lord, but only if you believe that it is imperative for me to be aware of such things."

Clasping her hands in front of her, Judith looked directly at Lord Turton, gazing into his dark grey eyes. Shadows bounced across his features, his brows low and a line forming between them.

"I believed, Miss Newfield, that this danger was gone. With the passing of my wife, I believed the matter closed. Now, it seems I was foolish to believe such a thing. The *ton* has become aware of my daughter, and thus the danger has now passed from my wife to her."

"Danger?" Judith bit her lip, glancing over to where Laura was merrily splashing her fingers in the fountain pond. "I do not understand, my Lord."

When she looked back at Lord Turton, he was gazing at her as though he had never seen her before. His eyes were a little narrowed, the darkness in his gaze piercing. His hands were held tightly behind his back and his stance was tall and strong. Uncertain as to why he looked at her with such intensity, Judith did all she could to look back at him directly, but found herself struggling with the fierceness of his gaze.

"Can I trust you, Miss Newfield?"

The low thrum of his voice sent Judith's heart into a frantic rhythm.

"I can be trusted, my Lord."

His eyes narrowed a little more and his jaw pulled tight. A few seconds ticked past, but Judith said nothing, waiting for his scrutiny of her to end.

Then he lowered his head. A long sigh escaped him, and Judith's heart began to settle itself once more.

"You care deeply for my daughter, Miss Newfield. That is something I cannot deny. I do not believe that you would ever knowingly put her in danger."

"No, my Lord, I would not. Nor would I ever do anything which would endanger you. I am trustworthy. I will not let you down."

Much to her astonishment, Lord Turton stepped forward, reached out one hand, and grasped one of hers. Another sigh broke from his lips, but this time, when he looked at her, there were no shadows in his eyes.

"I do trust you. Allow me to explain." Taking a deep

breath, Lord Turton moved even closer, his fingers now twining through hers, as though he needed to hold on to her as he spoke. "My marriage to my late wife was an arrangement. Looking back, I can see just how hasty it was, but at the time I was contented with the match. I wanted to make sure that my wife was happy and contented too, and for the first few months I believed her to be so. She was an excellent mistress of this house, and, after a short while, the doctor informed me that we were soon to be blessed with a child."

"Laura."

Lord Turton nodded.

"It was also at this time, however, that my wife approached me. She had received a letter from her father – Lord Granger – and, given that she was soon to bear our first child, she thought it best to tell me the truth."

He looked away and Judith saw his jaw work. Whatever he had to tell her was still a deep wound.

"Lord Granger had, not all that long before my betrothal to her, promised his daughter to another man. It was to be done in payment of a great debt. This gentleman, however, was naught more than a Baronet and, it appears, a gentleman of cruel character. Therefore, Lord Granger decided that his daughter should not be wed to such a callous fellow, despite the arrangement between them. And, so, with his agreement, she married me – she was unaware of that previous arrangement at the time. But our marriage caused dire consequences not only to my father-in-law but also to my wife."

Judith's eyes flared wide in horror.

"Sir George Huntley had been quite unaware of our marriage. Quite what Lord Granger had said, I am not certain, but evidently, he had said that the marriage between Huntley and his daughter would take place after a short delay. When Huntley heard that she was already wed, he threatened violence and retribution."

"I see."

Judith heard her voice rasping, evidence of the shock which began to course through her veins.

"Shortly thereafter, Lord Granger died. The last letter that he wrote to his daughter explained it all. His death was naught to do with Huntley, although that was my first suspicion. The gentleman had been unwell for some time and had not told his daughter. News of his passing was greatly troubling to us both. However, even during the mourning period, Huntley decided to enact his campaign of retribution against my wife."

Judith's eyes rounded.

"But what issue could he take with your wife?"

"He believed her a part of it. The letters which he sent to my wife after the passing of her father made it clear that he believed that she had deliberately escaped from her duty to him by marrying me instead."

"There was very little he could do, was there not?" Judith found herself gripping his fingers. "She was your wife. What could he expect from her?"

"I do not think that he expected anything. The man was – and is – blinded by anger and upset over what he believed he deserved and was deprived of. My wife was to be his as payment of a debt. When she did not become so, when Lord Granger refused to pay what he owed, for, as a man of honor, he had given what funds he had as her dowry, then Huntley practically lost his mind. Imagine a Baronet wed to Marquess' daughter! Think of the status which he could claim, and the standing in society which would be his! Her dowry would have been substantial also and, of course, her inheritance. When he learned that she was not to be his. he lost all sense. Letters began to come frequently. I declared to my wife that the man was reprehensible and even went to speak with him. But he threatened me with death should I step over his threshold." Closing his eyes, Lord Turton let out a long breath. "There was madness in his eyes, and I knew then, in my heart, that my dear wife was not safe with me any longer. When I returned home, the house was in an uproar. My wife had been out walking and had been attacked. Thankfully, she had been saved by the gardener – although he had been unable to apprehend the villain - and from that day I took him into my confidence. My wife, however, was much too afraid to go outside. Even though her injuries were minor, the threat of what could have happened hung over her head. I had been speaking with Huntley myself, at the time of the attack, so it could not have been him, personally, who attacked my wife. I realized then that the man had many in his command, ordering them to do as he desired without question. Many skulking shadows appeared in the gardens over the next few months. Letters continued to arrive from Huntley, threatening more and more. And so, I removed my wife from my house entirely."

Everything became clear in an instant. Judith closed her eyes, considering all that she had learned about Lady Turton and the danger both she and her unborn child had been in. Lord Turton had pulled himself from his wife and allowed her to live an entirely separate life so that she might be kept safe. That was why he had barely visited her. Of course, the rumor was that the child was not his and that, rather than face disgrace, he had sent his wife away, but Judith now realized the truth. Lord Turton had cared for his wife deeply. It was that care and consideration which had forced him to allow her to live an entirely separate life. A life where she would be safe.

"You understand Miss Newfield, I think."

"Yes, my Lord." Letting out a long breath, Judith looked back at him steadily. Their hands were still twined together, but she had no desire to break them apart. "It must have been a great torment for you to lose your wife when you had spent so little time with her."

Darkness flashed across his expression and his eyes became hooded.

"It is impossible for me to express the extent of my sadness, Miss Newfield. I kept my daughter there thereafter, in the hope that she too would be safe, whilst I confess, also attempting to take hold of my grief." Turning his head, he looked toward Laura. "I did not believe that Huntley would ever do anything to hurt my child, but now I believe I am mistaken. His desire for retribution has not been satisfied. Therefore, I must think of what to do to protect my daughter."

A sudden jolt of fear gripped Judith's heart.

"Do you mean to send her away?"

The heaviness in his expression tore at her.

"I do not know Miss Newfield." His words were heavy, his shoulders slumped. "I do not know what is for the best. I have told you that I wish to become a better, more present father, but how can I do so when she is far away? But how am I to protect her otherwise? If I go to speak to him again, I fear I shall never return. The man would already have his pistol prepared by the time I reached the front door of his house."

Judith shook her head.

"He sounds like a madman."

"He *is* a madman, but a madman with strength and

power. I could go with my own pistol but then what would happen? Either one or both of us would be killed and –"

"No, you cannot!" Before she knew what she was doing, Judith found her free hand suddenly clinging to Lord Turton's chest, her fingers burrowing into his shirt and crumpling his jacket. Her eyes were wide, and her breathing suddenly ragged as her heart slammed painfully against her chest. The horrific thought of little Laura being left without either parent had sent such a dagger into her heart that she had reacted without thinking. Lord Turton's eyes were huge with astonishment and his chest rumbled as he cleared his throat, turning his head a little so that he did not look into her eyes.

Mortified, Judith closed her eyes and dropped her hand, pulling her other one free from his. Stepping back, she shook her head, avoiding his gaze entirely. Heat seared her cheeks and nausea rose in her throat – a combination of both embarrassment and horror at what she had been told.

"You are thinking of Laura, of course."

Nodding, Judith kept her gaze low.

"I do not think that I ever expected you to have such a depth of feeling for my daughter after such a short time, Miss Newfield. Given the fact that you were pushed into this position without ever having an urge to do this kind of work, I believe that you are to be highly praised."

"Pray, do not." Swallowing hard against the hard lump which had formed in her throat, Judith shook her head. "I am quite useless. I cannot even give you a single thought about what you ought to do."

Lord Turton sighed, turning his head to look at his daughter as she continued to splash her fingers in the fountain. Judith turned with him, her heart aching.

"I will go with Laura, should you send her away." The

moment that she said it, Judith pressed both hands to her cheeks, aware of the flush of heat that had risen in her face again. "I beg your pardon, my Lord. What I meant to say was –"

"I quite understand." Lord Turton smiled at her and Judith's cheeks grew all the hotter. "Do not give even a single moment to the thought that I might send you away. I promise you that I will never do so. Your care and concern for my daughter are more than evident. You are the only person she has spoken to these last few months and that, Miss Newfield, speaks entirely for itself."

Even though her blush was furious, Judith dropped her hands and returned Lord Turton's smile.

"She is the most wonderful little girl, my Lord. I confess that the thought of being separated from her was torturous indeed."

Large Turton's smile faded.

"I wish I knew what else I might do. I do not want to send my daughter, nor you, away. I fear it would be of a long duration, and that separation is something I cannot abide."

Seeing Lord Turton's grimace and the pain creeping into the lines around his eyes, Judith took a long breath, studying him as she did so. The trust which he had placed in her was something she valued greatly and, therefore, Judith wanted to return that trust with something of significance.

"If you do not wish to send Laura away, my Lord, then you must find another solution. Perhaps I could help?" Lord Turton's eyes met hers, but he did not immediately refute the idea. "I am certain that, together, we could come up with a better alternative. It may take a little time, however."

"Time is something I have at present." A wry smile crossed his lips. "The house party is to end in three days. If I

– if *we* - cannot think of something else by that time, then I must make arrangements for Laura to be taken elsewhere."

A small flare of hope burned in Judith's chest, and she allowed it to lift the corners of her mouth.

"I am certain that we can find a solution in three days."

His hand reached out, settling on her shoulder, and then running lightly down her arm.

"You have more confidence than I, Miss Newfield, but I consider that a good thing."

Once more, his fingers caught hers and Judith shivered at the searing of her skin. Standing there in silence, holding on to his hand and looking into his eyes, she drew in a steadying breath, feeling a sense of closeness that had not been there before.

"I shall say nothing to Laura for the present. If that is what you think is best?"

Lord Turton squeezed her fingers, then dropped his hand. Turning, he looked back at Laura and his loud sigh rippled across to Judith.

"Yes, for the moment to tell her nothing. Let her enjoy the freedom which comes with ignorance."

Judith nodded.

"Given that she is so close to speaking as she once did, I would be loath to do or say anything which might push such progress back."

"Let us hope that it will be entirely unnecessary." Lord Turton smiled back at her, but Judith saw no flicker of hope in his eyes. "I must protect my daughter, Miss Newfield. No matter the cost to myself."

CHAPTER ELEVEN

David had to admit to a little surprise, seeing Lady Madeline and her mother still sitting at the dining table. Given that their betrothal was at an end, he had fully expected Lady Madeline to take her leave at once, but it seemed that the lady was stubborn and determined. She was not about to be shamed by him. Yes, her face was a little pale, but her eyes were bright, and she was laughing as she conversed with another gentleman. Her mother, on the other hand, had done nothing but glare at David from the very first moment that he had walked into the room. Even now, as he spoke to Lord Carr, David could feel her eyes upon him.

"Are the rest of the guests aware?"

Lord Carr nodded.

"Lady Madeline informed everyone this morning, once you had excused yourself from the dining room. She was very matter of fact. I will be honest and state that I was a little taken aback at her offhand manner."

"She made it seem that her betrothal, and its ending, was not of great importance?"

Lord Carr hesitated, tilting his head this way and that.

"More that she made it plain that she could find another person to marry very quickly indeed, should she wish it."

"And on that count, she is quite right." David shrugged. "I myself was one such person. Caught by her beauty, I proposed marriage before I was truly aware of her character."

Lord Carr nodded slowly, His eyes darting across the room to where Lady Madeline sat.

"She does not seem to be at all upset. When she was asked if she would stay for the remainder of the house party, her confirmation was given with such a manner of surprise that it was as though she had never even considered departing."

"I believe doing so would only prove to both myself and the rest of the guests just how eager she had been to marry." David let out a small sigh and shrugged again. "Lady Madeline has a beautiful face, but beneath it hides a multitude of dark shadows. After she struck Miss Newfield, I –"

Lord Carr's eyes widened in horror.

"She struck your governess?"

Grimacing, David confirmed it.

"She did and without due cause. I have insisted on the lady apologizing to Miss Newfield, but as yet she has not done so."

"Good gracious!" Lord Carr shook his head, pushing one hand through the hair flopping over his forehead. "There is more to the lady than I ever saw! I am glad for you that you have been able to find a way to escape her, although I do hope that it will not cause a great scandal. Could not the lady say whatever she wishes about you? What if she returns to London and spreads lies?"

"I have every certainty that she will not." A small sense

of pride lifted David's chin. "I did not threaten her, but needless to say, if she were to speak of me, then I would have no hesitation in speaking of her also."

A flare of understanding came into Lord Carr's eyes.

"That was wise. I do hope that this will be the end of the matter for you both. I pity whoever it is that she will, one day, come to marry." David's lips curved into a wry smile. "And is your governess quite well? She has not chosen to leave your household, I hope?"

"Because of Lady Madeline? No."

"That is good. The last thing you need is for your governess to disappear!"

David's lips fell into a flat, straight line. When he had walked with Miss Newfield that afternoon, all manner of emotions had been swirling through him. There had been uncertainty within him when it came to telling her the truth about what had happened in the past, and what was now, it seemed, affecting Laura's future. He had looked into her eyes and seen the openness and vulnerability there. She had trusted him by telling him the truth about her brother and her situation. It had been time for him to trust her also. David could see the deep affection she had for his daughter, and that touched his heart. When he had told her of the Baronet and his wicked schemes, he had seen fear throw itself into her features. Her eyes had strayed to Laura as though she wished to make certain she was safe from that very moment. Were he honest with himself, David would admit to a small twinge of fear within his own heart.

"Are you quite all right, old boy?" Lord Carr's face was filled with concern, his eyes searching David's features. "You have suddenly gone very pale indeed."

Letting out a slow breath, David shook his head.

"I am not all right. It appears that Huntley has returned." He did not need to give a further explanation for Lord Carr was already aware of the Baronet and all that had taken place. He watched as Lord Carr's eyes grew as round as saucers and his mouth fell open. "It is so," David confirmed to Lord Carr's silent question. "It must be. There have been men seen on the grounds. One of them attempted to approach Laura today when we were out in the gardens. Had I not been present, I dare not think about what might have happened." A tremor ran through him, but he stilled it with an effort, his hands curling into tight fists. "I have spoken with Miss Newfield. If I cannot find a way to end Huntley's determined attacks against my family, then I will have no other choice. I will have to send Laura away once more."

"Goodness." Lord Carr shook his head. "To send the girl away when she has only been at home for a short while..." Trailing off, he shook his head for the second time. "This is dreadful indeed."

"The governess is determined that we shall find another way forward." David could not keep the hopelessness out of his voice. "Alas, given that I have had no success previously, I cannot have the same faith."

"This governess appears to be of strong character." Lord Carr gave him a small smile, although his eyes were still filled with horror. "A trait that is not often seen in governesses."

"A trait I am more than grateful for." Letting his gaze move across his guests, David's heart sank low in his chest. "If we cannot find another solution by the time that the house party ends, then I will have no other choice but to make an arrangement for Laura and her governess to reside elsewhere. I have every trust in Miss Newfield. I know for a fact that she will be able to take care of Laura as though she were her own."

His friend smiled softly.

"That is a blessing. It appears as though you have found someone quite remarkable in this Miss Newfield!"

David's lips pulled upwards.

"Laura has spoken to her."

He did not need to say anything further for the astonishment in Lord Carr's face was more than obvious. For the second time, the man's mouth dropped open, but this time his eyes were filled with both happiness and delight rather than fear and dread.

"She has not yet spoken to me, more than a single word," he clarified before Lord Carr could say anything, "but that alone is remarkable, and I am certain that more will come in time." His flickering happiness died away. "Although mayhap it will never occur, if I am forced to send her away."

His friend put a comforting hand on David's arm.

"Let us pray it will not come to that. I am here. Whatever you need, I will do. I am certain that with the three of us, we will be able to find a way forward. Your daughter will remain here, and Huntley's schemes will come to an end."

"Would that I had your confidence." Sighing heavily, David forced a smile and turned to his other guests. "I suppose that I must continue as host. If we are to take a walk on the grounds, then we must do so very soon. It will become a little too cold for the ladies later."

Lord Carr put one hand out, stopping David from walking away.

"Did you not say that you saw a man on the grounds only yesterday?"

"I did, but I am certain the man will not return when

we are there as a group. Besides which, Huntley is only interested in my daughter. I believe his motives are to injure her or to take her from me so that I might feel the same loss as he supposedly felt."

"I do hope that Miss Newfield is keeping your daughter within the house!"

"She is permitted to walk out of doors, but only with supervision and a good deal of it!" David tried to smile. "My daughter does so love counting the fish in the pond."

Lord Carr hesitated, opened his mouth as though he wished to say something more, but then nodded and turned his head away. David sighed inwardly, reaching up to pinch the bridge of his nose with a thumb and finger.

I cannot lose hope.

Dropping his hand to his side, David took steadying breaths, straightening his shoulders as he did so. To lose hope would be to hand the victory to Huntley, to declare that he had won and that David himself would remain melancholy and fearful for Laura's safety for the rest of his life. Remembering the resolve in Miss Newfield's voice, David allowed that hope to flare in his own heart. Lord Carr was right. Surely with the three of them, they would be able to find a way to defeat Huntley's dark purposes for good.

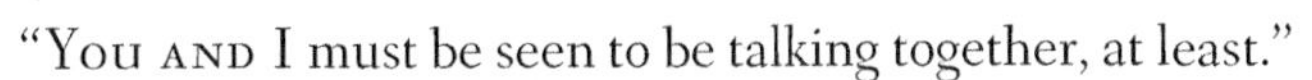

"You and I must be seen to be talking together, at least."

"Must we?" David barely glanced at Lady Madeline as they walked together across the gardens. "I believe that the rest of the guests would be more than understanding if we were to remain separated."

"And yet that is not what I wish."

Out of the corner of his eye. David saw the way that

Lady Madeline lifted her chin, her supercilious look rendering him more than a little frustrated. She had not considered whether or not *he* wished to speak with her but rather had forced her presence upon him.

"There is no need for the *ton* to gossip about us, more than they already will." Lady Madeline frowned; her lips pulled into a flat line. "How we act here will soon be reported in London."

"I care not."

Lady Madeline pouted.

"You think so little of me that you do not care what the *ton* might say."

"I care not because I will not be in London. And because I have realized that certain things are much more important than the whispers of scandal which will be spread by those who have nothing better to do than talk." David had not meant to speak harshly, but his words were thick with disdain. "Besides which, have you not been telling the other guests that you will soon find another to wed you? That the ending of our betrothal is not particularly significant to you?"

It took her a moment to respond, but when she did, her chin was already lifted and her eyes sparkling with a blazing fury.

"I say such things simply so that I do not appear injured! I make such remarks with confidence in the hope that I might not be left on the shelf! I have wasted a good deal of time upon you, Lord Turton. I do not think you understand in the least!"

David bit back his reply before he let it free. This was not the time for harsh words, particularly given that the other guests were a short distance from them.

"You know as well as I that you will not be left on the

shelf, Lady Madeline. There will be at least fifteen gentlemen back in London, eager to further their acquaintance with you.

Again, her rosebud lips pulled into a dislikeable pout. "But none will be a Marquess."

It was as if she had punched him in the stomach. David recoiled, his body curling gently as he came to a standstill. Lady Madeline did not so much as look back, she simply walked on, walking away from him, but David was certain that there would be a smile on her face. Her words had injured him, and she knew it. It was as if she wanted to retaliate against the ending of their betrothal, and had done so in the only way she knew how: by using harsh words against him.

She only ever considered me because I was a Marquess, because I am titled.

Nausea roiled in his stomach, and he was forced to catch his breath. His other guests were all walking ahead of him, and David took the opportunity to try to breathe at a normal rate so that his heart would stop pounding so fiercely. Lady Madeline had never said such a thing to him before, but now that he knew of her character, David had to admit that it would not be surprising if this was the truth.

Then she never had a genuine affection for me, not even a crumb.

"Lord Turton?" A quiet voice made him jump and he looked around. None other than Miss Newfield was peeking out from behind some bushes, and as he beckoned her over, she hurried out to join him. "Are you quite well?"

"Whatever are you doing here, Miss Newfield?" Refusing to answer her question, David's heart began to hammer furiously again as fear seared his heart. "My daughter, where is she?"

Miss Newfield touched his arm.

"Pray, do not be concerned, my Lord. I have left Laura in the care of one of the maids. She rose late this morning and is breaking her fast. I promised that I would go in search of some small flowers, whichever ones I can find at this time of year so that she might have a few on her table. I believe she thinks the schoolroom very drab indeed!"

David looked at her a little more closely. There was a redness about her eyes. Had she been crying? Was she afraid of being out here alone? His stomach twisted. Huntley's men would have seen the governess walking with Laura. She ought to be made aware of the danger.

"You could very well be a target for the Baronet also, Miss Newfield. You ought not to be out of doors without a companion, without someone to watch you."

"I do not believe that I am in any danger, my lord. To the Baronet – or to the men who serve him, I am only a servant."

David shook his head, unable to quell the growing concern rising in his heart.

"I could not lose you, Miss Newfield. I could not see you come to harm."

Her eyes widened slightly, and David grew more certain that she had been crying. The thought of Miss Newfield standing, weeping alone, was enough to rip his heart asunder.

"I do not think that such a thing would ever happen, Lord Turton. At present, I feel quite safe."

Taking a step forward, David shook his head, His hand reaching out to grasp hers tightly.

"I shall not risk it. You must have someone with you or be in sight of the gardener."

Looking down into her eyes, David felt his heart

quicken, but this time for an entirely different reason. His mouth went dry as the truth of what he felt began to fill his mind. This was more than just a protective instinct. This was more than just a master's responsibility to his staff - and that realization terrified him.

"I - I should return to the house." Miss Newfield gently began to pull her hand away. "I apologize if I have done wrong. I will not do so again."

David's heart and mind were filled with nothing more than the desire to go with her. In a single moment, he seemed to have forgotten entirely about his guests and his responsibility to them. He wanted now to explore what was within his heart, to realize the truth of it, and to let that settle within him.

She is, after all, the daughter of a Viscount. Were this in any other circumstance, then the furthering of our acquaintance would be quite proper.

Clearing his throat, David pulled her back towards him just a little, refusing to release her fingers.

"Perhaps we ought to talk again this evening."

"You have an entertainment planned for your guests, my Lord," she reminded him as a gentle flush crept across her cheeks. "An entertainment which requires your presence, I believe."

A dark frown pulled his brows low.

"Oh. yes, I had quite forgotten." Some time ago, when he had been planning for his house party, David had arranged for a small group of musicians to come and play, and he, as the host, was going to sing one or two songs with them. His guests would be delighted, he was sure, but at this moment David wished he had made any other arrangement than this. One eyebrow lifted gently as he studied her. "How might I ask, are you aware of such a thing?"

"Your daughter told me."

For a few moments, David did not realize the significance of what had been said. It was only when Miss Newfield began to laugh softly that he realized what she meant. It seemed that his daughter was able now to converse without hesitation.

"You mean to say that Laura is the one who told you of this evening's plans?" When she nodded, David's heart lifted to the skies. "She spoke to you directly? There was not only one single word?"

Miss Newfield spread her hands and began to laugh.

"I do not know how to explain it, my Lord!" Her eyes were brighter than he had ever seen them, the vivid blue and grey hues sparkling in the sunshine. "It was as though we have always had conversations. I was collecting the books which we would require for this morning's lessons, and when Laura appeared at the door, she immediately began to speak of what she had heard from the maid. I confess that I stared with such astonishment and delight that it took me some moments to reply!"

David did not know what to say. His throat constricted and he looked quickly away, not wishing her to see the moisture in his eyes. He realized now why Miss Newfield's eyes had been red-rimmed. She had been overwhelmed with the same joy that now spread through him.

I can hardly believe this. My daughter is finally restored.

"I cannot send her away." His voice was hoarse, but David did not care. "On hearing this, I know that I cannot send her from this house again. She is safe here. She is happy here, she is loved here. To remove her from all of this would be devastating indeed."

"Devastating for you both, I am sure."

David looked deeply into Miss Newfield's eyes. He

owed her so much. Since she had come to his house, since he had taken that risk in continuing to accept her position in his home as a governess, things had improved drastically. His daughter was speaking. She was happy. Miss Newfield *made* her happy. And her presence in the house had made David himself consider the sort of father he wanted to be. Yes, she had been outspoken. Yes, her words, at times, had cut him deeply, but David was grateful for all of it.

"I do not think that I have ever met a lady like you. Miss Newfield, you are the most kindhearted, compassionate, and outspoken young lady of my acquaintance!" Miss Newfield ducked her head. "I do not consider that quality to be a bad one." His voice was softer now as he took a small step closer. "Had you not been so blunt, had you not been so willing to speak to me with such honesty, then I might be considering sending her away for the second time. I certainly would have had no awareness of all that I would have missed out on, had I done so. I would have been lost in selfishness. I might even have still been betrothed to Lady Madeline!"

Miss Newfield shook her head, looking up at him with a wry glint in her eye.

"On that count, Lord Turton, I will not accept any praise."

"I shall insist that you do." A glowing warmth was beginning to settle in his heart. His thumb ran over the back of her hand as he smiled at her. He did not need time to consider what was in his heart, he was already aware of it. It was startling, astonishing, and altogether overwhelming, but David did not stumble back from it, nor push it away. It seemed to make complete sense, and he wanted to pull himself towards it – and toward Miss Newfield. It made very little difference to him that she was a governess and he a Marquess. These feelings were unlike anything he had ever experienced before. Yes, he had cared for his first wife, but love had not been a part of their commitment to each other. This, he realized, was what it felt like when the first shoots of love began to grow. "Do you not understand, Miss Newfield?" Wisps of red hair spun out from her temples, dancing in the light autumn breeze. Her blue eyes searched his, flecks of silver held within them. David did not think he had ever seen someone more beautiful. "It is true that I realized my betrothal to Lady Madeline was a mistake. I acknowledge that I acted hastily and that I was caught only by her beauty. But it was not just that. Lady Madeline herself has stated that I am much too caught up with you."

Sparks burned in her eyes.

"With me?"

"Yes, Miss Newfield, with you. Without realizing it, I have been thinking of nothing but you for some days. I have thought it was only concern for my daughter, and the situation at hand, but now that I am here, now that I am standing in front of you and looking into your eyes, I can see that there is something more. I can *feel* it, here." His free hand pressed against his heart, his heartbeat quickening as he stepped closer, still only an inch or two away from her. Her head tipped back slightly, her lips, a little parted. She did not lift a hand to press it lightly against his chest, nor drape it over his shoulder as Lady Madeline had done when he had first drawn close to her. There was no expectation. Instead, there was only shock. *I cannot push her.* "I have startled you, I can see that. I am an honorable man. Miss Newfield. There is nothing that is required of you."

She pressed her lips together, looking away.

"I fear you will ask me to depart."

"No, never! As I have just said, there is nothing

required of you. There is no expectation. I should never take you from my daughter, Miss Newfield. If there is a reciprocation of feelings, then I should be inclined to consider what I ought to do next but if there is not..." Even speaking of such a situation sent an arrow through his heart, making him flinch. "If there is not, then life will continue as it has always been. My daughter shall not be deprived of you."

Glistening tears began to form in Miss Newfield's eyes with one sparkling drop falling to her cheek.

"It is not appropriate for a governess to have any feelings for the master of the house."

"But you are not a governess. Miss Newfield. That is to say, you are a governess to my daughter, but you have not been in the past. You have been forced into this position by your brother, otherwise, you would be in society, thinking of going to London for the Season and perhaps breaking the hearts of many gentlemen there." A faint blush caught her cheeks, and she lowered her head. A swell of hope caught David's heart, as he realized that she had not said she felt nothing for him, only that it would be wrong for a governess to do so. "Miss Newfield."

Holding out one hand to her, he waited for her response and, after what felt like an age, she finally put her hand into his. Everything else seemed to fade away. The birdsong became quiet, the wind became still. When Miss Newfield lifted her head to look into his eyes, it was as though everything fell into the right place all at once. He did not need to pretend with the lady. He did not need to pretend to himself. Having rejected Lady Madeline entirely, David knew the sort of lady that he wished to have for his wife – a lady who was unafraid to speak her mind. A lady who cared deeply and quickly. A lady whose commitment to those she loved remained consistent and unending. A lady whose presence would convince him to be the very best husband and father he could be. The reason he found Miss Newfield so extraordinary was because there was none like her. In the face of Lady Madeline's arrogance and self-centeredness, he had found someone precisely the opposite. Someone who did not complain about her brother's ill treatment, but someone who sought to do their best regardless of circumstances.

"I - I am afraid, Lord Turton."

A quiet chuckle escaped him.

"Then you find me in the very same circumstance, Miss Newfield. I too am afraid, and a trifle uncertain. But one thing I am convinced of is that I do not wish you to ever depart from my life."

The tears in her eyes were not pushed away by her smile. Instead, they increased all the more, but David prayed that they came from a place of joy. With their hands joined. David moved to pull her close, only to be interrupted by a shout from behind him.

"The ladies are cold, Turton. Are you to show us this rose garden or shall we step back inside?"

Grimacing, David turned around, dropping Miss Newfield's hands as he did so.

"I shall join you in a moment."

Lord Carr nodded, his eyes drifting to where Miss Newfield stood, her head bowed. His gaze returned to David, and he gave him a small swift nod as though silently offering his approval.

"I must beg your forgiveness. Miss Newfield, and return to my guests. Perhaps we can continue this conversation at a later time."

"Yes, of course, I quite understand."

As she went to turn around, to walk away from him,

David reached out and grasped one of her hands, catching her a little off guard. Lifting it to his mouth, he dropped a kiss on the back of it, aware of the heated stirrings in his belly. He did not want to kiss her hand, but rather her mouth, but that time was still to come. Reminding himself that he would not press her, David reluctantly released her hand and stepped back, dropping into a low bow.

"Do excuse me, Miss Newfield."

She did not respond to him but rather, immediately began to turn away. Her face was a little flushed, but her eyes would not meet his. Letting out a hiss of breath, David stepped even further back, bringing an end to their nearness, and sending a heaviness into his heart. They had been on the cusp of something monumental, he was sure of it – but it had been snatched from him before it could be realized.

And that was most frustrating indeed.

CHAPTER TWELVE

Judith turned away from the window, letting a heavy sigh fall from her lips. It was the final evening of the house party and, try as she might, Judith could not help but feel a little jealous. Even in the schoolroom, she could hear the music from the ballroom echoing up towards her. Her mind was filled with thoughts of Lord Turton dancing, taking various young ladies in his arms as he stepped out with them. It was not the fact that she was missing the ball, Judith realized, but more that she was missing Lord Turton. She wanted to be where he was. After she had met him in the garden yesterday afternoon, Judith could tell that something had changed between them. The way he had spoken to her, the truth he had revealed to her, had been more than astonishing. She had never expected the Marquess to tell her that his heart belonged to her, and thus, had been entirely uncertain as to how to respond. When he had asked her what she felt for him, Judith had been unable to give him the answer he required. Stumbling and stuttering, she had given him a poor excuse about how governesses ought not to feel anything for the master of the house. Instead of being vulnerable, instead of being open, she had struggled against both.

And then the opportunity to be entirely honest with him had been snatched away. Judith knew that if he had gone to kiss her, she would have responded in kind. In fact, she had longed for him to do so. He had been so close to her; he had been so very near that she had believed the kiss imminent. There would have been no way to hide her feelings had he touched his lips to hers.

But what does that mean for my position here?

Biting her lip, Judith closed her eyes and took in a deep breath. She ought to trust that Lord Turton would do nothing to harm her residence here nor the connection she had to his daughter – but that fear lingered regardless. If she had admitted to him all that she felt, then would her position as governess have become untenable? And if they began a courtship, then what would happen to Laura? Judith could not be a governess and court Lord Turton at the same time.

"All the same, I should like to dance with him."

Another sigh broke from her lips, but Judith straightened and continued to tidy up the schoolroom. For the moment at least, she was still the governess, and that meant that she had duties and responsibilities. At least now, she was certain that Lord Turton would not send Laura away, and that was a great relief indeed!

"Miss Newfield?"

A tiny voice caught Judith's attention and she straightened, turning around to see none other than Laura standing in the doorway.

"My dear girl, whatever are you doing here?"

Laura, clad in her nightgown and with bare feet, gave a small shrug.

"I could not sleep. The music is rather loud."

Judith smiled, thinking silently to herself that there was probably more to this than just genuine sleeplessness.

"Come in and close the door so that you do not catch a chill." Setting down some books on her desk, Judith smiled at Laura as she came a little further into the room. "Do you know that, when I was young, I often could not sleep when my father threw a ball?"

Laura's eyes widened.

"Truly?"

Judith laughed.

"Yes, indeed! But it was not the music that kept me awake, but rather a deep wish to join them. I wanted to see the ladies dressed in all their finery. I wanted to see the gentlemen stepping out with them to dance! I wanted to hear the music, to watch the orchestra play, and perhaps even have a little of the refreshments!" Laura began to giggle, and Judith tilted her head, looking at her charge with a sharp eye. "Might it be that you are thinking something similar, my dear?"

"I think I must be. Oh, Miss Newfield. is there any way that I might watch some of the ball?"

Taking a deep breath, Judith considered.

"I have not received your father's permission."

"Could you not ask him?"

Judith chuckled.

"Given that he is probably dancing, I hardly think that it would be a wise idea to interrupt him."

"I am certain that he would not mind."

The excitement in little Laura's eyes was too much for Judith to ignore.

"If you return to your bed and promise that you will stay there until I return, then I shall find a way to ask your father. Although," she continued quickly, as Laura clapped her hands together in excitement, "you must also be prepared for him to say no."

This warning seemed to make very little difference to the child, for she let out a little yelp of delight and then rushed to the door.

"I will return to my bedchamber this minute!"

Judith laughed and shooed her out of the door before following. Making certain that Laura was back in her bedchamber, she turned and made her way to the stairs. Quite what she was going to do to garner Lord Turton's attention, Judith was not sure. The last thing she wanted to do was to make him angry or frustrated with her, but yet the light in Laura's eyes forced her to act.

The only noise Judith could hear was the music from the ballroom, floating up towards her. The rest of the house appeared quite empty, and there were not even any staff around. No footman stood by the doors, no maid scurried from place to place. It was a rather strange feeling to be the only person walking through the main part of the house and, as Judith approached the staircase, her hand gripped the banister a little more tightly than was required.

Before she could begin her descent, however, the front door suddenly opened. It was a slow and steady movement that Judith did not immediately notice, until the creak which echoed up towards her alerted her to the fact that she was no longer alone.

She stopped, hesitated, then turned to walk back to the top of the stairs. If it was a guest, then Judith did not want to be seen. It would be best for her to find a footman or a maid who could speak to Lord Turton on her behalf. It would not be wise for a governess to enter a ballroom.

Her heart leaped in her chest as Judith watched the front door of the house open still further – and after a moment or two, caught sight of a man skulking at the doorway. He did not come in, he did not go out. Instead, he stood by the door and peered around it. Judith's instincts told her that this was no guest. He was not meant to be here. Fear clutched at her heart, and she almost turned on her heel to run back to Laura's room, only to realize that she, at present, was the only one who knew that this man was here. Her heart began to hammer furiously in her chest as she fought to know what was best to do. Her instincts told her to return to Laura, to make sure that the child was safe. But, on the other hand, she had a responsibility to Lord Turton to inform him of this man's presence in his house. Yes, there was the fear that Laura was the target of Sir George Huntley's ire, but what if the man went to Lord Turton instead? If she did nothing, then Judith knew that she would be responsible for whatever occurred thereafter.

"Oh, Miss Newfield. I beg your pardon, I did not see you standing there."

Judith spun on her heel, her eyes wide. Holding one finger to her lips, she grabbed the maid's arm and dragged her back into the shadows in the hallway.

"Christie, there is something I must ask you to do."

"Is something the matter, Miss Newfield?" Judith could see the alarm growing in the maid's eyes. "Whatever is the trouble?"

"You must go to Laura's room at once. Do not frighten her but go in with her and then lock the door behind you. The key is in its usual place."

Christie blinked rapidly.

"I do not understand."

"I must go to speak to Lord Turton at once, but I must make certain that Laura is not alone. Promise me that you will do this at once."

Her hand gripped the maid's tightly and after a few moments, Christie nodded.

"Yes, Miss Newfield. Although someone will have to tell the housekeeper why I'm absent from my duties!"

"You will not have any trouble, I swear it to you. Lord Turton will be more than grateful." Releasing the maid's hand, Judith stepped back and gestured to the hall. "You must go now. And remember to lock the door."

Christie nodded and scurried off into the dark, leaving Judith to stand alone. Fear crawled across her skin like a spider, but she stepped forward to the stairs once more. As silently as she could, she stood, and her eyes searched the hallway below.

There.

The man had come in fully, shutting the door behind him. Judith shrank back as his gaze began to tilt towards the stairs, seeing him clinging to the shadows as best he could. He was dressed in the finest suit, but every movement was slow and careful, as though he was terrified of being seen. Judith had no doubt where his steps were headed. He was making his way to the ballroom.

Is there a way for me to be there before him?

Frantically, her mind guided her through the different paths she could take to reach the ballroom first.

And then she ran.

Turning away from the stairs, she rushed towards the other end of the house, knowing that she could use the servants' stairs to go below and then back up again. The music of the ballroom no longer seemed warm and welcoming, but rather frenzied and panicked, pushing her towards her goal. Her lungs burned as she gasped for air, her heart slamming hard against her ribs. Various footmen and maids stepped out of her way or sent her an odd look, but Judith did not care. Without having any time nor requirement to explain, Judith rushed to the other end of the servant's hall and climbed up the next set of stairs.

"Excuse me, excuse me!"

Behaving in a more ill-mannered fashion than she had ever done in her life before, Judith elbowed maids out of her way as she climbed to the top of the stairs. She was closer now, but without any idea as to where this intruder might be. Silently, Judith prayed that she would reach Lord Turton before him, terrified of what would take place if she did not.

"You cannot go in, Miss Newfield." One of the footmen by the door of the ballroom moved to block her path, his arms folded across his chest. "Surely you are aware that a governess would not attend such a function."

Judith dragged in air.

"I am not attending. I come to warn Lord Turton and if you stand in my way, then you will be responsible for whatever evil befalls him thereafter."

The footman's eyes flared wide, but Judith did not give further explanation. Instead, she moved forward with purpose, ignoring his astonished expression. Her eyes lifted to his and, after a moment, the footman moved out of her way. Hurrying past him, Judith was just about to enter the ballroom before another thought struck her. Turning back, she grasped the footman's arm.

"There is a man here. I do not know his name nor his purpose, but he has not been invited to the ball. I fear he will attempt to join the other guests for he both looks and will act as one of them. Do not allow him in."

Without another word, Judith turned and made her way into the ballroom. Pushing the doors open, she stepped into the clamor and the heat, with one single purpose in mind.

Where is Lord Turton?

"Whatever is the meaning of this?" High pitched, angry words threw themselves in Judith's direction. "Whyever are *you*, the governess, here this evening?"

Cold fingers wrapped around Judith's upper arm, pulling her back.

"If you will excuse me."

Judith did not want to explain to anyone, least of all to Lady Madeline, and attempted to pull her arm away, but the lady was determined to cling on to her.

"You think much too highly of yourself, Miss Newfield. You think that because you are often in Lord Turton's company, he thinks well of you?"

The cruel laugh which shook through Judith's frame from the point of Lady Madeline's grip did nothing but add to her tension. Again, she tried to pull her arm away, but Lady Madeline clung on with determination. Her grip was rather painful, and Judith winced, uncertain of what she ought to do next. She did not want to embarrass herself, nor embarrass Lord Turton since she was a member of his staff, but the need to remove herself from Lady Madeline's company was ever present and growing steadily.

"I have good reason to be here." Keeping her voice low, Judith looked directly into Lady Madeline's eyes. "I will depart again in a moment, but only once I have spoken to Lord Turton."

"A governess has no reason to speak to the master at a ball," Lady Madeline laughed, her lip curling. "No doubt you hoped for a few moments here amongst the invited guests, reminding yourself of what it used to be like when you were in society."

Her words stabbed at Judith's heart. Holding herself very still, she looked up into the lady's face, aware of the chill which now flooded her. Every moment that Lady Madeline held her back was another moment for the unknown gentleman to walk into the ballroom and find Lord Turton.

"It is moments like these, Lady Madeline, that remind me of the things I do not miss about society. I do not miss the coldness, the cruelty, and the arrogance of those who think that they are better than everyone else around them simply by virtue of their title or their wealth." Keeping her head lifted, she held fast to Lady Madeline's gaze. "Now, you will release me so that I may go and speak to Lord Turton and then return to my position which, Lady Madeline, I know very well indeed."

Lady Madeline's beautiful features were suddenly darkened. Her lips twisted to one side and her eyes narrowed as she pulled Judith close.

"I would not hesitate to strike you again, were it not for the fact that I would certainly gain Lord Turton's ire for such an action."

"You certainly would." Lord Turton's deep voice broke between them, and Judith let out a breath of relief. Attempting to turn towards him but still held fast by Lady Madeline, she sent the lady a hard glare. Eventually, Lady Madeline's fingers released her arm. "Whatever is the meaning of this?" Lord Turton frowned but did not appear to be angry. "Miss Newfield. Is there something wrong? Is it Laura?"

"It is not Laura. She came to ask me if she might come to watch the ball for a few moments. She claimed she cannot sleep due to the music, but I believe it is mostly excitement. I confess, Lord Turton, that I was quickly convinced, given her anticipation and eagerness."

His frown grew all the more.

"And you thought simply to come into the ballroom and ask me?"

Something like shame began to curl in her belly, but Judith dismissed it quickly. Now was not the time to consider her own feelings.

"I am aware that as a governess, I ought to remain above stairs. I should not like you to think otherwise. Lord Turton. However, I thought to ask a footman to go in search of you so that I might have the opportunity to speak with you privately about your daughter's request. That thought was quickly dismissed when I noticed someone arriving at the house." Her heart began to clatter again, and she made to reach out for him, only to pull her hand back. With Lady Madeline watching on, she could not be indiscreet. "I do not believe Lord Turton, that the gentleman I saw enter through the front door has been invited to your ball this evening."

In an instant, his eyes flared, and the color drained from his cheeks. Evidently, he understood.

"Where is my daughter?"

His voice was hoarse, but Judith grasped his hand, squeezing it hard before releasing it again.

"A maid is with her, and the door is locked. It was not in the direction of her rooms that the gentleman came, however. He was making his way to the ballroom. In fact, I believe he may already be here."

"Gentleman?"

Lady Madeline's high-pitched voice interrupted their conversation, and both Judith and Lord Turton turned to her at once.

"This matter does not concern you, Lady Madeline. Excuse me."

Lord Turton turned on his heel and beckoned Judith forward.

"I spoke to the footman at the door, my Lord. I begged him to be on his guard and, while I did not give him much of an explanation, I believe that he will be careful to only admit those with an invitation."

"Most of my guests are already here." Lord Turton threw her a dark glance. "You say that he arrived only some minutes ago?"

Judith nodded.

"I came a different way to the ballroom, in the hope of preceding him."

"That was very wise, Miss Newfield. Once more, it seems, I am to be filled with gratitude for you."

Judith pressed her lips together as Lord Turton pushed open the door to the ballroom.

"You need not thank me yet, my Lord."

One of the footmen caught the door and held it open for them both - only for Lady Madeline's voice to reach their ears once more.

"This is preposterous! You cannot show such interest in a governess!"

"This does not concern you, Lady Madeline. Return to the ball!" Swinging around to face her, Lord Turton slashed the air between them with one hand. "There is no need for your presence here. We do not need your meddling!"

"And I will not be cast aside so that you might take up with the governess!" Lady Madeline exclaimed, throwing her hands in the air. "You may pretend that there is some grave matter which concerns you both, but I am all too aware of the truth of the situation."

Judith shook her head.

"You know nothing, Lady Madeline, what you are saying is entirely untrue."

"And I cannot oblige you with further explanations, not at the present moment." Turning smartly, Lord Turton approached one of the footmen, clearly expecting Lady Madeline to return to the ballroom as he had asked. "Have you allowed any gentleman entry since Miss Newfield spoke to you?"

The footman shook his head.

"No, my Lord." His eyes caught Judith's for a moment. "I did not mean to hold Miss Newfield back. I did not understand that there was –"

"You need not explain," Judith put in. "Lord Turton, if the man has not appeared, then that must mean that he is yet to arrive at this door- unless it is that he has decided not to come to the ballroom after all."

"Who is it you are speaking of?" Lady Madeline's harsh words echoed toward them, but both Lord Turton and Judith ignored her. "I will not be disregarded! I..."

Suddenly aware that Lady Madeline had trailed off, Judith turned towards her as Lord Turton muttered to himself, one finger pressed lightly against his lips. Much to Judith's surprise, Lady Madeline had gone sheet white. Her eyes did not meet Judith's, but rather looked over her shoulder to something beyond.

"Lady Madeline, what -?"

"Stop!"

Lord Turton's voice echoed down the hallway, startling her. Twisting her head back, she saw a man approaching them, his hands clasped loosely behind his back. Her heart began to hammer furiously, and she pressed one hand hard against her stomach. This was the same man that she had seen enter the house only a short while ago, she was certain of it.

"Forgive me, Lord Turton, but I do not have an invitation."

The man's voice was mild, and he showed no sign of anger. As Judith studied him, she was taken aback at his gentle expression. His gaze was soft, and his lips pulled into a half-smile. Was this all a pretense? Was it a show, meant to encourage them to trust him before he did something terrible?

"What is your name, sir?" Lord Turton moved to stand directly in front of the man. "And why is it that you have entered my house without an invitation? What possible reason could there be for such an intrusion?"

Judith watched the man's eyes shift slightly and, at that moment, suddenly everything seemed to make sense. Letting out a long breath of relief, she took a small step forward.

"You are not here to frighten or intimidate Lord Turton, nor are you here to injure his daughter."

The man's eyes widened, and he held both hands up in a defensive gesture.

"I have no intention of harming anyone." He dropped his hands. "I can only apologize if that is what you believed my intention to be. I confess that I had not even thought of such an outcome."

Judith saw Lord Turton's shoulders relax in evident relief, matching her own feelings.

"Then you have not been sent by Sir George Huntley?"

In answer to Lord Turton's question, the man shook his head.

"No, I have not. I am not even acquainted with such a gentleman."

Judith put one hand on Lord Turton's arm.

"My Lord, I believe that I understand." Glancing back at Lady Madeline, she saw her eyes begin to flood with tears. "I think that Lady Madeline is acquainted with this gentleman."

Slowly, Lord Turton's gaze made its way from Judith to Lady Madeline. When he finally faced her, Lady Madeline turned her head away, but not before Judith saw a single tear fall to her cheek.

"Lady Madeline." Lord Turton's voice was gentle, as though he sensed that this situation was causing her a great deal of distress. "Do you know this man?"

For a moment, Judith was afraid that Lady Madeline would deny all knowledge of him, even though his presence was clearly having an effect on her. Even from where she stood, Judith could see her trembling. Lady Madeline's lips pinched, and she opened her mouth to say something – only to throw a glance towards the gentleman and then drop her head. Her hands went to her eyes and her shoulders began to shake.

"This is not the place for such a discussion." Lord Turton shook his head, clearly aware that something very strange was going on. "I am confused about all that has occurred, but at the very least, I am certain that my daughter is not in any immediate danger and that comes as a great relief."

"She is not in any danger from me, I promise you," the man added, clearly eager to make his intentions plain. "I thought only of Lady Madeline. I can only apologize for interrupting your ball in this manner, Lord Turton, but I had no other choice."

A strangled sob came from Lady Madeline's throat, and Judith's heart tore for her. Despite all that Lady Madeline had done, despite all of the cruelty which she had shown towards her, Judith could not help but feel sympathy for her. There was a great turmoil going on within the lady's heart – a torment that, as yet, she had never spoken of, or explained to anyone. It was very troubling indeed for, even at this point, Lady Madeline was entirely unable to do anything other than weep. Putting her arm gently around Lady Madeline's shoulders, Judith threw a questioning look toward Lord Turton. He understood her immediately.

"Perhaps you might take Lady Madeline to the drawing-room, Miss Newfield?"

Judith nodded

"And you might also send for tea?" she suggested. "I am sure that Lady Madeline would appreciate such a thing."

Lady Madeline did not respond. Her shoulders continued to shake, and Judith led her quietly away, leaving Lord Turton and the other gentleman - whose name they still did not know - to talk alone.

CHAPTER THIRTEEN

"You are exceedingly kind. Miss Newfield. After how I have treated you, you surely ought to be unwilling to do even the smallest thing for me."

"No, not at all."

Pulling out her handkerchief from her sleeve, Judith handed it to the lady just as a maid set down the tea tray.

"I am sorry for striking you, Miss Newfield."

It was the apology that Lord Turton had demanded from his then-betrothed and, despite the circumstances, Judith appreciated her words deeply. She smiled softly.

"Thank you, Lady Madeline."

In only a matter of minutes, Lady Madeline had gone from a proud, determined, confident young lady to a shadow of her former self. Her eyes were red, and her tears had not stopped falling since they had entered the drawing-room. Judith's tongue was tied with questions, but she did not permit herself to ask a single one. This matter did not concern her, and even though she was involved in a small way, Judith knew she would need to step aside and return to her duties with Laura.

"I am sorry to see you in such distress." Reaching for the teapot. Judith poured a second cup for Lady Madeline. "I do not know where Lord Turton has gone, but I am certain that he will join us very soon."

"And will think all the more ill of me, given what I have done."

Lady Madeline dropped her head into her hands and once more her shoulders began to shake.

"I am certain it cannot be as bad as you think it." Setting down the teacup in front of Lady Madeline, Judith tried to give her a warm smile of encouragement when she lifted her head. "Lord Turton is nothing if not forgiving. I should know, given that I have made matters rather difficult for him on more than one occasion."

"I can hardly believe that, Miss Newfield." Lady Madeline's voice was shaking. "From what I have seen, he has sought out your company in a way that he never sought out mine."

"That is only because I am his daughter's governess." Judith reminded her, gently. "I have had much to discuss with him as regards his daughter."

Lady Madeline lifted her eyes and gazed back at Judith. There was a question in her eyes which Judith could not answer. Turning her head away, she felt a faint blush creep up into her cheeks as her mouth went dry.

"I can tell that it is a little more than that. Miss Newfield." A small sigh escaped from Lady Madeline's lips. "But I shall not hold that against you, although I am deeply upset over the ending of our betrothal. I do not like to admit this but, in my heart, I know that it is for the best, particularly now that I have seen him again."

Judith could not begin to understand what it was that Lady Madeline meant by such a remark. Yes, she could question, yes, she could ask what it was that the lady meant - but for the moment she chose to remain silent. She herself had not admitted to all that she felt for Lord Turton but that, it seemed, did not need to be said either. The door opened and Judith rose quickly, a little relieved that they had been interrupted.

"Please, be seated."

Lord Turton walked into the room, gesturing for her to seat herself.

There is no need for me to do so, my Lord," Judith protested, gesturing to the tea "Lady Madeline has all that she requires. I must return to my duties."

Lord Turton closed the door tightly, then turned back to face her. Silver poured into his grey eyes as a gentle smile caught his mouth, making Judith's blush return. The tenderness with which he looked at her was more than apparent - and she was afraid that Lady Madeline could see it also.

"You need not return to your duties. Miss Newfield. I apologize for my tardiness, but I thought it best to go to my daughter. I wanted to make sure, not only that she was safe, but that she had the opportunity to spend some minutes at the ball." Upon hearing this, such a warmth filled Judith that it spread to the very tips of her fingers and toes. her heart soared to the skies. It was proof that Lord Turton cared deeply for his daughter and wanted to make her a part of his life. "I confess it was a little unusual to be carrying and spinning my daughter around the dance floor, and certainly a good many of the guests gave me questioning looks, but to hear her laughter and to see her smile made my heart sing for joy." He gestured to Judith. "Had you not become my daughter's governess, I do not think that I should ever have done such a thing. Miss Newfield." A gently teasing smile twitched across his lips. "But, given that this is my house and given that I am the host of this ball, I believe I can do whatever I wish. I relished those minutes with my daughter, and I fully intend to spoil her from this day forward!"

Clasping her hands together. Judith closed her eyes for a moment, a soft smile settling across her face.

"I am very glad to hear it, my Lord. I am sure that Laura will speak of nothing else come the morrow."

"I look forward to hearing what she has to say," came the reply. "But now, please do seat yourself. There are some things which we must all discuss." Waiting until Judith had taken her seat, Lord Turton made his way back to the door, opened it, and stepped back. After a moment, the unknown gentleman walked into the room. His eyes were fastened on Lady Madeline, but the lady responded to his gaze by merely dropping her head. "Miss Newfield. Might I present Viscount Stratford."

Judith rose and dropped into a quick curtsey.

"How good to make your acquaintance, Lord Stratford."

"Good evening, Miss Newfield." The man put his hand to his heart. "I am sorry for frightening you so. Lord Turton has explained the circumstances, and there is much that I must apologize for."

Judith merely nodded, and then took her seat again. She did not fully comprehend what Lord Stratford meant, but again, did not think it her place to ask any questions. At this moment, she was not a Viscount's daughter sitting amongst equals; she was governess to Lord Turton's daughter. Lord Stratford took a seat close to Lady Madeline, leaning forward in his chair so that he might see into her eyes.

"Will you not look at me, Madeline?" Again, Lady Madeline refused to look at him, but her cheeks were steadily warming. "There is no need to pretend." Lord

Stratford reached out and touched Lady Madeline's hand. "Lord Turton knows all."

Lady Madeline's eyes flew to Lord Turton's as Judith watched, trying her best to understand when only snippets of information were given.

"I do not confess to know everything, but from what I have been told, I understand that this man is deeply in love with you, Lady Madeline." Lord Turton spoke gently, and Lady Madeline dropped her head into her hands once more. "You turned from him, even though you had promised him your heart."

"I did not wish to." Lady Madeline's words were broken by sobs. "My mother insisted that I do so, and my father was quite adamant."

"But you knew that I wished to elope. I was there, waiting for you, Madeline. The carriage was prepared. The horses were ready to run. But you did not come."

Judith turned her attention to Lord Turton, not wishing to gaze at Lord Stratford and Lady Madeline, for it felt almost as though she were intruding on their privacy. His grey eyes were already watching her, and a tiny smile tugged at one edge of his mouth.

He is relieved.

"Wait a moment!" Judith's exclamation left her lips before she could prevent it. Shock and embarrassment mingled together, bubbling up into her core but she did not stop. "I understand now. You were the man in the garden, were you not?"

Wide eyes fixed themselves to Lord Stratford, and when he nodded, Judith let out such astonished exclamation of relief that Lord Turton began to laugh.

"You have reacted in the very same manner as I did, only a short while ago, Miss Newfield," he said, as Judith stared fixedly at Lord Stratford. "The man you saw scurrying across the grounds, the man who ran when I gave chase - they were one and the same." He indicated Lord Stratford with a nod of his head. "He was not pursuing Laura as we had feared."

"Indeed, I was not." Lord Stratford spoke urgently, as though he wished to absolve himself of any wrongdoing. "I had not seen either Lord Turton or yourself, Miss Newfield. I was afraid that the child was out walking alone and intended to make certain of her safety. It was foolish of me to run away when Lord Turton came towards me, but I did not want to give any explanation about who I was or to account for my presence in his gardens."

The relief which swamped Judith was so overwhelming that she could not speak. There had been nothing to fear, after all. There was no Sir George Huntley here. His men were not pursuing Lord Turton, seeking to injure him. Laura was safe, and there was no concern about her being separated from her father again. Everything was just as it ought to be, and, as she wrapped her arms about her waist and dragged in a breath, Judith wanted to weep aloud with relief and joy.

"What were you doing in the gardens?" Lady Madeline spoke quietly, her eyes searching Lord Stratford's face. "Why have you been skulking around Lord Turton's home?"

Lord Stratford smiled softly, leaning forward once more, and reaching out to take Lady Madeline's hand. Lady Madeline did not pull away, but rather held his gaze, watching him as though the answer he would give would lead her to either hope or to darkness.

"To see you, my dear lady - but I knew that your mother would not approve of my presence. I did not know if your father was here also, but were he to even see me, I was certain that he would have thrown me from the house. I was not an invited guest and, therefore, I could not simply march to the front door, knock on it, and insist on seeing you. If I am to be truthful, I was uncertain of whether or not you would even come to speak with me, had I had the courage to do such a thing."

Lady Madeline's eyes fluttered, and she looked away.

"I want to marry you." Lord Stratford leaned closer still, his words soft and full of an unmistakable love for the lady before him. "I know that you have been unhappy. The betrothal to Lord Turton was not your decision. Yes, you accepted him, but was it not that both your mother and your father insisted that you do so, should he ask?"

Judith's eyes widened as Lady Madeline began to nod. Yes, Lady Madeline's character was severely lacking in some parts, but to see her as she was now, broken and sorrowful, told Judith that some of her behavior had stemmed from a great and unspoken pain – the pain of a broken heart.

"I am sorry, Lord Turton." Lady Madeline looked up at him, her eyes glistening with fresh tears. "I accepted you and pretended that I was filled with nothing but delight about our betrothal. The truth of the matter is that I was forced to do so. I wanted to marry Lord Stratford, but my father refused to give his permission. They insisted that a diamond of the first water could do better and that a mere Viscount was not enough of a title. When you sought to court me, I had no other choice but to accept. My evident joy and happiness was nothing but an act. I confess that my heart has always belonged to another, even though I did not think I would ever see him again." Tears fell to her cheeks, but her smile was bright.

"But now that he has returned to me, he has fought for me, and I cannot help but go back to him." So saying, Lady Madeline turned to Lord Stratford with a warm, beautiful smile that lit up her features. "If you prepare another carriage, Lord Stratford, then this time I will not fail you."

A thrill of hope run up Judith's spine.

"You are to wed?"

"If I can get us to Gretna Green, then yes." Lord Stratford rose to his feet, taking Lady Madeline with him. "Lord Turton, after all that I have done thus far, I must now beg to intrude upon your hospitality a little more."

Judith got to her feet, just as Lord Turton rose and stuck out one hand to shake that of Lord Stratford.

"By all accounts, I ought to insist that Lady Madeline return to the ball and that you depart this house," he began, although a broad grin settled across his face as he spoke. "However, I am not a gentleman inclined to stand in the way of such a beautiful thing as this. I will speak to a footman at once and a carriage will be ready within the hour." He gave Lady Madeline a quick smile. "Lady Madeline, I suggest that you return to the ballroom and tell your mother that you need to retire early. If she is not looking for you already, then she certainly will begin to wonder where you are very soon."

Lord Stratford nodded, putting one arm around Lady Madeline's shoulders, and gently pulling her close. The lady bit her lip, her face a little white.

"What if she is able to tell -?"

"She will not be able to tell a thing," Lord Stratford interrupted, smiling at her. "Go, my dear lady. I will see you within the hour."

Judith watched as Lady Madeline nodded, smiled, and

then finally walked to the door. Passing Lord Turton, she dropped into a curtsey, her hand reaching out to take his.

"Thank you, Lord Turton."

The gentleman bowed in return.

"But of course, Lady Madeline. I wish you both every happiness."

"AND NOW, THEY ARE GONE." Judith let out a long breath as she and Lord Turton continued to watch out of the window. "This has been a most extraordinary evening."

A deep rumbling laugh came from Lord Turton's chest.

"Indeed, Miss Newfield! Most extraordinary."

Not at all embarrassed. Judith laughed with him, her eyes holding fast to the dim lantern lights of the carriage as it continued to drive away.

"Do you think that they will be interrupted?"

Lord Turton shook his head and Judith let out a sigh of relief.

"You are glad for her?"

"Yes, of course I am. She was given an opportunity for happiness and was forced to turn from it. It was not her wish to do so, but she had no other choice. Now, however, she has that opportunity again and I am extremely glad indeed that she has grasped at it with both hands – and that Lord Stratford was willing to fight for it."

"Do you think him a courageous man?"

Considering for a few moments, it took Judith a second to nod.

"Yes, I do. He listened to his heart, and he chose to fight for what he wanted. He did not give up, not even in the face of despair and doubt. That, I think, makes him a very courageous gentleman indeed." A small smile lifted her lips and she let out a contented sigh. "The way he declared himself to Lady Madeline was quite wonderful. He did not hide what he felt, but told her directly. I believe that, in the end, *that* is what convinced her to go with him." Taking a deep breath, she made to turn away from the window. "I should now return to my rooms. You have your guests and your ball to consider, and I would not like to delay you any longer."

Much to her astonishment, Lord Turton grasped her arm and as she turned to look up at him, stepped closer.

"And what would you think of me, Miss Newfield, if I declared *myself*?"

Her heart immediately tore into a furious rhythm as she looked up into his face and saw the question lingering in his dark grey eyes.

"I... I should think you courageous also, my Lord."

Her voice was softer now, no longer holding the confidence with which she had spoken only a few moments ago. Sparks were shooting up her arm from where he held her, and everything within her began to cry out to move closer to him. Was what they had shared the previous day in the garden now to come to fruition?

"Then I will declare myself, Miss Newfield." Both hands rested on her shoulders, then began to slide down her arms towards her hands. "I confess that my heart is yours. I confess that as master of this house, I feel such extraordinary things for my daughter's governess, to the point that I must ask her to reconsider her position here."

Her eyes widened, her breath swirling in her chest as fear began to rip through her heart.

"Are you sending me away?"

This was not what she had thought he had intended and certainly was not what she had thought he would say. A dark and angry heat dropped from her head to her shoulders, to her stomach, and then to her toes. Perhaps all of this had been a very great mistake.

But then, Lord Turton's fingers twined with hers. His other hand lifted to her cheek, his thumb brushing lightly along her jawline, and all of Judith's fears died in an instant.

"I should never send you away. I do not think I could bear it, should you be parted from me. I ask you to reconsider your position here, Miss Newfield, wondering whether or not you would accept the position as mistress of this house."

It took Judith a moment to realize what he meant but, when she finally did so, her shock was so great that a loud, audible gasp broke free of her lips. Every single part of her began to burn with an extraordinary sensation as sparks twisted this way and that. Lord Turton chuckled and then slipped both hands around her waist, pulling her closer to him than ever before.

Judith could not catch her breath. Her hands pressed lightly against Lord Turton's chest as she looked up into his eyes and saw how he smiled at her. That familiar tenderness was back in his expression and Judith felt it wrap around her very soul.

"You are asking me to become your bride?"

Lord Turton nodded.

"I am, Miss Newfield. I will confess to you now that, when I first proposed to Lady Madeline, I felt none of what I feel now. It was a foolish endeavor, and brought us both a great deal of trouble."

"Trouble which has been resolved now, at least."

Grinning, Lord Turton's arms tightened a little more around her waist.

"Precisely, Miss Newfield. Lady Madeline has found

the one her heart loves and I believe that I have found mine." His smile faded as he spoke with great solemnity. "I have come to love you, Miss Newfield. You are extraordinary. Your honesty, your sweetness, your kindness, and your gentle nature have overwhelmed me, to the point that I could not live a single day without you."

Her heart lifted in her chest and Judith found her hands slipping around Lord Turton's neck. Her fingers brushed through his dark hair, and she smiled at the ragged breath that such an action drew from him.

"I am certain that you are already aware that I return your feelings," she answered softly. "I have battled against them, given my position in your household, but they would not leave me."

His lips met hers suddenly in a gentle yet fiery kiss. They did not linger for long, but the heady sensations which poured through Judith at even the brief touch was enough to overwhelm her. A sigh broke from her lips and her hands tightened gently around his neck as Lord Turton's lips brushed her forehead. Happiness blossomed like a beautiful flower that had been waiting for just the right moment to show the world its bloom, and Judith leaned her head back, ready to give him his answer.

"I will reconsider my position, Lord Turton." The teasing in her voice made him chuckle, but the brightness in his eyes was unmistakable. "So long as I do not have to be parted from either yourself or from Laura, then I am very willing indeed to take on such a role."

"Then you shall make me the happiest man in all of England," came the fervent reply. "I love you most dearly, Judith, and swear to do so for the rest of my days."

. . .

I HOPE you enjoyed Judith's story. She did much better than I would as a governess and I am glad she ended up with a lovely little girl and a kind husband who loves her. If you missed the first book in the Ladies on their Own series, check out More Than a Companion. Read ahead for a sneak peak of the story!

MY DEAR READER

Thank you for reading and supporting my books! I hope this story brought you some escape from the real world into the always captivating Regency world. A good story, especially one with a happy ending, just brightens your day and makes you feel good! If you enjoyed the book, would you leave a review on Amazon? Reviews are always appreciated.

Below is a complete list of all my books! Why not click and see if one of them can keep you entertained for a few hours?

The Duke's Daughters Series
The Duke's Daughters: A Sweet Regency Romance Boxset
A Rogue for a Lady
My Restless Earl
Rescued by an Earl
In the Arms of an Earl
The Reluctant Marquess (Prequel)

A Smithfield Market Regency Romance
The Smithfield Market Romances: A Sweet Regency Romance Boxset
The Rogue's Flower
Saved by the Scoundrel
Mending the Duke
The Baron's Malady

The Returned Lords of Grosvenor Square

The Returned Lords of Grosvenor Square: A Regency Romance Boxset

The Waiting Bride

The Long Return

The Duke's Saving Grace

A New Home for the Duke

The Spinsters Guild

The Spinsters Guild: A Sweet Regency Romance Boxset

A New Beginning

The Disgraced Bride

A Gentleman's Revenge

A Foolish Wager

A Lord Undone

Convenient Arrangements

Convenient Arrangements: A Regency Romance Collection

A Broken Betrothal

In Search of Love

Wed in Disgrace

Betrayal and Lies

A Past to Forget

Engaged to a Friend

Landon House

Mistaken for a Rake

A Selfish Heart

A Love Unbroken

A Christmas Match

A Most Suitable Bride

An Expectation of Love

Second Chance Regency Romance
Loving the Scarred Soldier
Second Chance for Love
A Family of her Own
A Spinster No More

Soldiers and Sweethearts
To Trust a Viscount
Whispers of the Heart
Dare to Love a Marquess
Healing the Earl
A Lady's Brave Heart

Ladies on their Own: Governesses and Companions
More Than a Companion
The Hidden Governess
The Companion and the Earl
More than a Governess

Christmas Stories
Love and Christmas Wishes: Three Regency Romance Novellas
A Family for Christmas
Mistletoe Magic: A Regency Romance
Heart, Homes & Holidays: A Sweet Romance Anthology

Happy Reading!

All my love,

Rose

A SNEAK PEEK OF MORE THAN A COMPANION

PROLOGUE

"Did you hear me, Honora?"

Miss Honora Gregory lifted her head at once, knowing that her father did not refer to her as 'Honora' very often and that he only did so when he was either irritated or angry with her.

"I do apologize, father, I was lost in my book," Honora replied, choosing to be truthful with her father rather than make excuses, despite the ire she feared would now follow. "Forgive my lack of consideration."

This seemed to soften Lord Greene just a little, for his scowl faded and his lips were no longer taut.

"I shall only repeat myself the once," her father said firmly, although there was no longer that hint of frustration in his voice. "There is very little money, Nora. I cannot give you a Season."

All thought of her book fled from Honora's mind as her eyes fixed to her father's, her chest suddenly tight. She had known that her father was struggling financially, although she had never been permitted to be aware of the details. But not to have a Season was deeply upsetting, and Honora had to immediately fight back hot tears which sprang into her eyes. There had always been a little hope in her heart, had always been a flicker of expectation that, despite knowing her father's situation, he might still be able to take her to London."

"Your aunt, however, is eager to go to London," Lord Greene continued, as Honora pressed one hand to her stomach in an attempt to soothe the sudden rolling and writhing which had captured her. He waved a hand dismissively, his expression twisting. "I do not know the reasons for it, given that she is widowed and, despite that, happily settled, but it seems she is determined to have some time in London this summer. Therefore, whilst you are not to have a Season of your own – you will not be presented or the like – you will go with your aunt to London."

Honora swallowed against the tightness in her throat, her hands twisting at her gown as she fought against a myriad of emotions.

"I am to be her companion?" she said, her voice only just a whisper as her father nodded.

She had always been aware that Lady Langdon, her aunt, had only ever considered her own happiness and her own situation, but to invite your niece to London as your companion rather than chaperone her for a Season surely spoke of selfishness!

"It is not what you might have hoped for, I know," her father continued, sounding resigned as a small sigh escaped his lips, his shoulders slumping. Honora looked up at him, seeing him now a little grey and realizing the full extent of his weariness. Some of her upset faded as she took in her father's demeanor, knowing that his lack of financial security was not his doing. The estate lands had done poorly these last three years, what with drought one year and flooding the next. As such, money had been ploughed into the ground to restore it and yet it would not become profitable again for at least another year. She could not blame her father for that. And yet, her heart had struggled against such news, trying to be glad that she would be in London but broken-hearted to learn that her aunt wanted her as her companion and nothing more. "I will not join you, of course," Lord Greene continued, coming a little closer to Honora and tilting his head just a fraction, studying his daughter carefully and, perhaps, all too aware of her inner turmoil. "You can, of course, choose to refuse your aunt's invitation – but I can offer you nothing more than what is being given to you at present, Nora. This may be your only opportunity to be in London."

Honora blinked rapidly against the sudden flow of hot tears that threatened to pour from her eyes, should she permit them.

"It is very good of my aunt," she managed to say, trying to be both gracious and thankful whilst ignoring the other, more negative feelings which troubled her. "Of course, I shall go."

Lord Greene smiled sadly, then reached out and settled one hand on Honora's shoulder, bending down just a little as he did so.

"My dear girl, would that I could give you more. You already have enough to endure, with the loss of your mother when you were just a child yourself. And now you have a poor father who cannot provide for you as he ought."

"I understand, Father," Honora replied quickly, not wanting to have her father's soul laden with guilt. "Pray, do not concern yourself. I shall be contented enough with what Lady Langdon has offered me."

Her father closed his eyes and let out another long sigh, accompanied this time with a shake of his head.

"She may be willing to allow you a little freedom, my dear girl," he said, without even the faintest trace of hope in his voice. "My sister has always been inclined to think only of herself, but there may yet be a change in her character."

Honora was still trying to accept the news that she was to be a companion to her aunt and could not make even a murmur of agreement. She closed her eyes, seeing a vision of herself standing in a ballroom, surrounded by ladies and gentlemen of the *ton*. She could almost hear the music, could almost feel the warmth on her skin... and then realized that she would be sitting quietly at the back of the room, able only to watch, and not to engage with any of it. Pain etched itself across her heart and Honora let out a long, slow breath, allowing the news to sink into her very soul.

"Thank you, Father." Her voice was hoarse but her words heartfelt, knowing that her father was doing his very best for her in the circumstances. "I will be a good companion for my aunt."

"I am sure that you will be, my dear," he said, quietly. "And I will pray that, despite everything, you might find a match – even in the difficulties that face us."

The smile faded from Honora's lips as, with that, her father left the room. There was very little chance of such a thing happening, as she was to be a companion rather than a debutante. The realization that she would be an afterthought, a lady worth nothing more than a mere glance from the moment that she set foot in London, began to tear away at Honora's heart, making her brow furrow and her lips pull downwards. There could be no moments of sheer enjoyment for her, no time when she was not considering all that was required of her as her aunt's companion. She would have to make certain that her thoughts were always fixed on her responsibilities, that her intentions were settled on her aunt at all times. Yes, there would be gentlemen to smile at and, on the rare chance, mayhap even converse with, but her aunt would not often permit such a thing, she was sure. Lady Langdon had her own reasons for going to London for the Season, whatever they were, and Honora was certain she would take every moment for herself.

"I must be grateful," Honora murmured to herself, setting aside her book completely as she rose from her chair and meandered towards the window.

Looking out at the grounds below, she took in the gardens, the pond to her right and the rose garden to her left. There were so many things here that held such beauty and, with it, such fond memories that there was a part of her, Honora had to admit, which did not want to leave it, did not want to set foot in London where she might find herself in a new and lower situation. There was security here, a comfort which encouraged her to remain, which told her to hold fast to all that she knew – but Honora was all too aware that she could not. Her future was not here. When her father passed away, if she was not wed, then Honora knew that she would be left to continue on as a companion, just to make certain that she had a home and enough coin for her later years. That was not the future she wanted but, she considered, it might very well be all that she could gain. Tears began to swell in her eyes, and she dropped her head, squeezing her eyes closed and forcing the tears back. This was the only opportunity she would have to go to London and, whilst it was not what she had hoped for, Honora had to accept it for what it was and begin to prepare herself for leaving her father's house – possibly, she considered, for good. Clasping both hands together, Honora drew in a long breath and let it out slowly as her eyes closed and her shoulders dropped.

A new part of her life was beginning. A new and unexpected future was being offered to her, and Honora had no other choice but to grasp it with both hands.

CHAPTER ONE

Pushing all doubt aside, Robert walked into White's with the air of someone who expected not only to be noticed, but to be greeted and exclaimed over in the most exaggerated manner. His chin lifted as he snapped his fingers towards one of the waiting footmen, giving him his request for the finest of brandies in short, sharp words. Then, he continued to make his way inside, his hands swinging loosely by his sides, his shoulders pulled back and his chest a little puffed out.

"Goodness, is that you?"

Robert grinned, his expectations seeming to be met, as a gentleman to his left rose to his feet and came towards him, only for him to stop suddenly and shake his head.

"Forgive me, you are not Lord Johnstone," he said, holding up both hands, palms out, towards Robert. "I thought that you were he, for you have a very similar appearance."

Grimacing, Robert shrugged and said not a word, making his way past the gentleman and finding a slight heat rising into his face. To be mistaken for another was one thing, but to remain entirely unrecognized was quite another! His doubts attempted to come rushing back. Surely someone would remember him, would remember what he had done last Season?

"Lord Crampton, good evening."

Much to his relief, Robert heard his title being spoken and turned his head to the right, seeing a gentleman sitting in a high-backed chair, a glass of brandy in his hand and a small smile on his face as he looked up at Robert.

"Good evening, Lord Marchmont," Robert replied, glad indeed that someone, at least, had recognized him. "I am back in London, as you can see."

"I hope you find it a pleasant visit," came the reply, only for Lord Marchmont to turn away and continue speaking to another gentleman sitting opposite – a man whom Robert had neither seen, nor was acquainted with. There was no suggestion from Lord Marchmont about introducing Robert to him and, irritated, Robert turned sharply away. His head dropped, his shoulders rounded, and he did not even attempt to keep his frustration out of his expression. His jaw tightened, his eyes blazed and his hands balled into fists.

Had they all forgotten him so quickly?

Practically flinging himself into a large, overstuffed armchair in the corner of White's, Robert began to mutter darkly to himself, almost angry about how he had been treated. Last Season he had been the talk of London! Why should he be so easily forgotten now? Unpleasant memories rose, of being inconspicuous, and disregarded, when he had first inherited his title. He attempted to push them aside, but his upset grew steadily so that even the brandy he was given by the footman – who had spent some minutes trying to find Lord Crampton – tasted like ash in his mouth. Nothing took his upset away and Robert wrapped it around his shoulders like a blanket, huddling against it and keeping it close to him.

He had not expected this. He had hoped to be not only remembered but celebrated! When he stepped into a room, he thought that he should be noticed. He *wanted* his name to be murmured by others, for it to be spread around the room that he had arrived! Instead, he was left with an almost painful frustration that he had been so quickly forgotten by the *ton* who, only a few months ago, had been his adoring admirers.

"Another brandy might help remove that look from your face." Robert did not so much as blink, hearing the man's voice but barely acknowledging it. "You are upset, I can tell." The man rose and came to sit opposite Robert, who finally was forced to recognize him. "That is no way for a gentleman to appear upon his first few days in London!"

Robert's lip curled. He should not, he knew, express his frustration so openly, but he found that he could not help himself.

"Good evening, Lord Burnley," he muttered, finding the man's broad smile and bright eyes to be nothing more than an irritation. "Are *you* enjoying the London Season thus far?"

Lord Burnley chuckled, his eyes dancing - which added to Robert's irritation all the more. He wanted to turn his head away, to make it plain to Lord Burnley that he did not enjoy his company and wanted very much to be free of it, but his standing as a gentleman would not permit him to do so.

"I have only been here a sennight but yes, I have found

a great deal of enjoyment thus far," Lord Burnley told him. "But you should expect that, should you not? After all, a gentleman coming to London for the Season comes for good company, fine wine, excellent conversation and to be in the company of beautiful young ladies – one of whom might even catch his eye!"

This was, of course, suggestive of the fact that Lord Burnley might have had his head turned already by one of the young women making their come out, but Robert was in no mood to enter such a discussion. Instead, he merely sighed, picked up his glass again and held it out to the nearby footman, who came over to them at once.

"Another," he grunted, as the man took his glass from him. "And for Lord Burnley here."

Lord Burnley chuckled again, the sound grating on Robert's skin.

"I am quite contented with what I have at present, although I thank you for your consideration," he replied, making Robert's brow lift in surprise. What sort of gentleman turned down the opportunity to drink fine brandy? Half wishing that Lord Burnley would take his leave so that he might sit here in silence and roll around in his frustration, Robert settled back in his chair, his arms crossed over his chest and his gaze turned away from Lord Burnley in the vain hope that this would encourage the man to take his leave. He realized that he was behaving churlishly, yet somehow, he could not prevent it – he had hoped so much, and so far, nothing was as he had expected. "So, you are returned to London," Lord Burnley said, making Robert roll his eyes at the ridiculous observation which, for whatever reason, Lord Burnley either did not notice or chose to ignore. "Do you have any particular intentions for this Season?"

Sending a lazy glance towards Lord Burnley, Robert shrugged.

"If you mean to ask whether or not I intend to pursue one particular young lady with the thought of matrimony in mind, then I must tell you that you are mistaken to even *think* that I should care for such a thing," he stated, plainly. "I am here only to enjoy myself."

"I see."

Lord Burnley gave no comment in judgment of Robert's statement, but Robert felt it nonetheless, quite certain that Lord Burnley now thought less of him for being here solely for his own endeavors. He scowled. Lord Burnley might have decided that it was the right time for him to wed, but Robert had no intention of doing so whatsoever. Given his good character, given his standing and his title, there would be very few young ladies who would suit him, and Robert knew that it would take a significant effort not only to first identify such a young lady but also to then make certain that she would suit him completely. It was not something that he wanted to put his energy into at present. For the moment, Robert had every intention of simply dancing and conversing and mayhap even calling upon the young ladies of the *ton,* but that would be for his own enjoyment rather than out of any real consideration.

Besides which, he told himself, *given that the* ton *will, no doubt, remember all that you did last Season, there will be many young ladies seeking out your company which would make it all the more difficult to choose only one, should you have any inclination to do so!*

"And are you to attend Lord Newport's ball tomorrow evening?"

Being pulled from his thoughts was an irritating interruption and Robert let the long sigh fall from his lips without hesitation, sending it in Lord Burnley's direction who, much to Robert's frustration, did not even react to it.

"I am," Robert replied, grimacing. "Although I do hope that the other guests will not make too much of my arrival. I should not like to steal any attention away from Lord and Lady Newport."

Allowing himself a few moments of study, Robert looked back at Lord Burnley and waited to see if there was even a hint of awareness in his expression. Lord Burnley, however, merely shrugged one shoulder and turned his head away, making nothing at all of what Robert had told him. Gritting his teeth, Robert closed his eyes and tried to force out another long, calming breath. He did not need Lord Burnley to remember what he had done, nor to celebrate it. What was important was that the ladies of the *ton* recalled it, for then he would be more than certain to have their attention for the remainder of the Season – and that was precisely what Robert wanted. Their attention would elevate him in the eyes of the *ton*, would bring him into sharp relief against the other gentlemen who were enjoying the Season in London. He did not care what the gentlemen thought of him, he reminded himself, for their considerations were of no importance save for the fact that they might be able to invite him to various social occasions.

Robert's shoulders dropped and he opened his eyes. Coming to White's this evening had been a mistake. He ought to have made his way to some soiree or other, for he had many invitations already but, given that he had only arrived in London the day before, had thought it too early to make his entrance into society. That had been a mistake. The *ton* ought to know of his arrival just as soon as was possible, so that his name might begin to be whispered amongst them. He could not bear the idea that the pleasant notoriety he had experienced last Season might have faded already!

A small smile pulled at his lips as he considered this, his heart settling into a steady rhythm, free from frustration and upset now. Surely, it was not that he was not remembered by society, but rather that he had chosen the wrong place to make his entrance. The gentlemen of London would not make his return to society of any importance, given that they would be jealous and envious of his desirability in the eyes of the ladies of the *ton*, and therefore, he ought not to have expected such a thing from them! A quiet chuckle escaped his lips as Robert shook his head, passing one hand over his eyes for a moment. It had been a simple mistake and that mistake had brought him irritation and confusion – but that would soon be rectified, once he made his way into full London society.

"You appear to be in better spirits now, Lord Crampton."

Robert's brow lifted as he looked back at Lord Burnley, who was studying him with mild interest.

"I have just come to a realization," he answered, not wanting to go into a detailed explanation but at the same time, wanting to answer Lord Burnley's question. "I had hoped that I might have been greeted a little more warmly but, given my history, I realize now that I ought not to have expected it from a group of gentlemen."

Lord Burnley frowned.

"Your history?"

Robert's jaw tightened, wondering if it was truly that Lord Burnley did not know of what he spoke, or if he was saying such a thing simply to be a little irritating.

"You do not know?" he asked, his own brows drawing low over his eyes as he studied Lord Burnley's open expression. The man shook his head, his head tipping gently to one side in a questioning manner. "I am surprised. It was the talk of London!"

"Then I am certain you will be keen to inform me of it," Lord Burnley replied, his tone neither dull nor excited, making Robert's brow furrow all the more. "Was it something of significance?"

Robert gritted his teeth, finding it hard to believe that Lord Burnley, clearly present at last year's Season, did not know of what he spoke. For a moment, he thought he would not inform the fellow about it, given that he did not appear to be truly interested in what they spoke of, but then his pride won out and he began to explain.

"Are you acquainted with Lady Charlotte Fortescue?" he asked, seeing Lord Burnley shake his head. "She is the daughter of the Duke of Strathaven. Last Season, when I had only just stepped into the title of the Earl of Crampton, I discovered her being pulled away through Lord Kingsley's gardens by a most uncouth gentleman and, of course, in coming to her rescue, I struck the fellow a blow that had him knocked unconscious." His chin lifted slightly as he recalled that moment, remembering how Lady Charlotte had practically collapsed into his arms in the moments after he had struck the despicable Viscount Forthside and knocked him to the ground. Her father, the Duke of Strathaven, had been in search of his daughter and had found them both only a few minutes later, quickly followed by the Duchess of Strathaven. In fact, a small group of gentlemen and ladies had appeared in the gardens and had applauded him for his rescue – and news of it had quickly spread through London society. The Duke of Strathaven had been effusive in his appreciation and thankfulness for Robert's actions and Robert had reveled in it, finding that his newfound status within the *ton* was something to be enjoyed. He had assumed that it would continue into this Season and had told himself that, once he was at a ball or soiree with the ladies of the *ton*, his exaltation would continue. "The Duke and Duchess were, of course, very grateful," he finished, as Lord Burnley nodded slowly, although there was no exclamation of surprise on his lips nor a gasp of astonishment. "The gentlemen of London are likely a little envious of me, of course, but that is to be expected."

Much to his astonishment, Lord Burnley broke out into laughter at this statement, his eyes crinkling and his hand lifting his still-full glass towards Robert.

"Indeed, I am certain they are," he replied, his words filled with a sarcasm that could not be missed. "Good evening, Lord Crampton. I shall go now and tell the other gentlemen here in White's precisely who you are and what you have done. No doubt they shall come to speak to you at once, given your great and esteemed situation."

Robert set his jaw, his eyes a little narrowed as he watched Lord Burnley step away, all too aware of the man's cynicism. *It does not matter,* he told himself, firmly. *Lord Burnley, too, will be a little jealous of your success, and your standing in the* ton. *What else should you expect other than sarcasm and rebuttal?*

Rising to his feet, Robert set his shoulders and, with his head held high, made his way from White's, trying to ignore the niggle of doubt that entered his mind. Tomorrow, he told himself, he would find things much more improved. He would go to whatever occasion he wished and would find himself, of course, just as he had been last Season – practically revered by all those around him.

He could hardly wait.

JOIN MY MAILING LIST

Sign up for my newsletter to stay up to date on new releases, contests, giveaways, freebies, and deals!

Free book with signup!

Facebook Giveaways! Books and Amazon gift cards!
Join me on Facebook: https://www.facebook.com/rosepearsonauthor

Website: www.RosePearsonAuthor.com

Follow me on Goodreads: Author Page

You can also follow me on Bookbub!
Click on the picture below – see the Follow button?

Rose Pearson